4/ru

# FAITHFUL

NAN A. TALESE

DOUBLEDAY

NEW YORK   LONDON   TORONTO   SYDNEY   AUCKLAND

# FAITHFUL

A NOVEL

DAVITT SIGERSON

PUBLISHED BY NAN A. TALESE
AN IMPRINT OF DOUBLEDAY
a division of Random House, Inc.

DOUBLEDAY is a registered trademark of Random House, Inc.

This book is a work of fiction. Names, characters, businesses, organizations, places, events, and incidents either are the product of the author's imagination or are used fictitiously. Any resemblance to actual persons, living or dead, events, or locales is entirely coincidental.

*Book design by Gretchen Achilles*

Library of Congress Cataloging-in-Publication Data
Sigerson, Davitt.
Faithful : a novel / Davitt Sigerson.— 1st ed.
p.   cm.
1. Man-woman relationships—Fiction.
2. Relationship addiction—Fiction.
3. London (England)—Fiction.
4. New York (N.Y.)—Fiction.   I. Title.
PS3619.I47F35 2004
813'.6—dc21            2003048890

ISBN 0-385-51050-0

PRINTED IN THE UNITED STATES OF AMERICA

April 2004

FIRST EDITION

1   3   5   7   9   10   8   6   4   2

# FAITHFUL

PART ONE

ick Clifford watches the fan sweep a white ceiling, looks down into the vortex of white sheets, and smiles at his Möbius strip of a milk white girl. An undersea swirl of straight black hair. A light, mouth-breathing sleep. Gaudí seashell feet, the heels round, unflattened, no evidence of weight bearing because she skips, she floats, she glides. Nearest to him is the right little toe, curved slightly toward the others. Nick imagines running a fingernail down the sole, imagines the foot curling in response, the unconscious grasp, the pinks pinker, a reef alive with baby suction. A waking stretch, the foot touches Nick on the side of his head, and Trish is up, laughing.

"Oh, it's you!" And she's gone, skimming the cool floor to the bathroom. Yes, him, betrothed a fortnight ago, wed three nights since, honeymooned with Trish's free miles on this island, sunny and unexplored. Done it over and over, as his seed seized each chance to make the connection between them be forever.

This afternoon they fly home. Tomorrow morning Nick will go back on the trading floor to get his back slapped and drinks bought. Why did she marry him, he wonders, as her shower covers the cicadas with white noise. Because for once God smiled his way. Once, and that's good enough. Tomorrow morning the wife will be stepping out of a black cab at Heathrow for her five days to Dubai and back, pointing her Eurobusiness prospects around the tax-advantaged paradise. They must go for the whole slim deal of her—fawn legs, tight waist, brave little bosom—and fall into those kind blue eyes. The white noise stops. She showers quickly, a habit from her boarding school days.

Bouncing back into the room, smiling like a kid. As she passes, Trish gives an angled tap to the stalks of velvety seaweed, already losing their submarine orange, that she has rescued and stuck in a milk bottle washed ashore. Nick smiles too, reminded of how his father could focus the telly with one flick on the rabbit ears. She will bring clarity and beauty to his life.

Trish flops on the bed, rooting for him, giggling and gobbling. Yes, it's God he must thank, to grant him even a taste of this. Gin and spare time helped: but how could it have become four weeks from just four hours? She saw his good heart. Finally someone did, and valued it. Which is what got her to the Chelsea Town Hall? That's a lot of credit on a good heart. The dick fattens in her mouth. Must let the wife do the work this time, she's the boss. Still, he can say I love you as much as he wants now, and he wants to.

But it's Trish who sighs, "Oh Nick. I'm so happy." And then, "No messing about! We've got a plane to catch!"

She works her filthy ingenuities. Pop pop pop. The stopper bounces inside his soul and the empty ache empties again.


IT IS NICE TO BE OFF TO WORK on a drizzling February Monday, nice to resent the cold and damp, nice to fight the stuffed and soggy smells of the Northern Line, and that familiar eerie one of burning. Up the long moving staircase and out into the gray squalor of the City. The Exchange isn't inherently beautiful. It's neither old nor elegant, charming nor charmless. It is a monument to the sensible working out of competing desires. Here the humors are veined, the passions brokered, rationalized in the fast congress of seller and buyer. The coveted thing, and the quantity of it, and the long or short of it, exist on both sides of the trade, as either possession or desire. Until the contract struck by these men fixes meaning to all the words: a price. Offered, accepted: a hypothesis until set, the price is reality, as real as and equal to and defining the thing itself. In a life-giving thunderclap, the entire package—the thing, its worth, to whom and when—becomes true. And true again, a newer truth, a moment later, and many times over, before lunch. Only the traders understand this power of theirs, to make truth. Perhaps others, grief-stricken men, look for a lasting kind.

At dinner the boys stand him, insist on Dom, hollering and clapping. Those who have met Trish leer in flattery. Most offer platitudes. These men find nasty stuff to say about almost everyone, but with Nick they don't try. Nick is liked here, not for wit or wealth or any exceptionality, but simply because he is so cheerful and sharp, a pillar of this society, always ready to promote a piss-up, just as prepared to get down to work again when it comes time.

The way home is lighter, drier, and not as acrid as the way down. Nick lets himself into his flat, now their flat. Many kinds of married homecoming—arriving with her from their honeymoon yesterday, arriving to find her there, or out—are already familiar. Trish is drinking vodka and cranberry with some Midlands managing director high above a featureless desert. With her away, Nick feels more than ever married, more than ever that her essence has saturated his rooms, his things, his sleep.

The place in West Hampstead is anonymously agreeable. But by being where Trish's sweaters fill a bureau drawer, Trish's cotton puffs from Boots sit on a ledge by the sink, Trish's family pictures now rule the parlor from a small table, Nick's flat has become his home through the force of its becoming hers. The arrival of Trish's bottle of Vichy Milk Moisturiser has changed reality in a way beyond what they do at the Exchange. Like incense swaying down the aisle in church, unlocking centuries of memory, the smell of her sanctifies the place. Suddenly many things are true. And though the details will change, the truth of these moments remains true, forever. Whatever happens, wherever they may go, this will have been their home, and they are husband and wife here, at this time for all time.

How good is his memory? Suppose the L-1011 Allah Cruiser plunges into the Red Sea? For how long could he retain her? The smell would still be here, but it's mostly Diorella. Yes, he will always associate it with her, and granted it isn't Diorella neat, rather Diorella plus Trish. Could he remember her breath, deliciously boozy, molasses and juniper? Could he remember her ears? He walks to the ashtray atop the bureau: little pearl earrings with a tiny diamond each. Presents from a spurned lover? He pulls the stem from the back of one and draws it through his thumb and forefinger. He puts his fingers to his nose. Girl sweat, and a memory of figs. But other girls' earrings are just as sweet—in fact, the same.

OK, go to work. Into the hamper, and out comes the white cotton shirt from last Thursday's wedding party. Perfume again, but now the Diorella and the girl are each more distinct. She must have put some on, then put the shirt on, then sprayed more on the inside, below the collar probably. There are two Trish smells: the frank faint traces of proper sweat under the arms—righteously girly, but not exclusively Trish—and then another one, around the trunk; subtler, more entwined with the Diorella, and more essential. Smelling it makes him think powerfully of her. And though it won't stay just as it is now, this will be the smell that he and their children and their grandchildren will think of when they think of what it's like to be hugged by Trish.

Next item: the black hair tie, a stretchy woven ring. Past the cigarette smoke, the Diorella, the shampoo, he thinks he can detect something fundamental; he's not sure. Back to the hamper and out comes a pair of white ankle socks: nice but again not *sui generis*. And the knickers. The back, the front: strong generic flavors, still, like any girl's.

So what has he got, and what would he have in two weeks if she died tonight, past a few loads of laundry? He'd have Diorella, he'd have the DNA to reconstruct anyone he's ever fucked, a white girl between sixteen and forty, but not Trish. By nose alone he sees he can't hold her.

NICK GOES TO THE COOPER'S ARMS, his local, for a supper of sausage and chips. Trish would tease him, but Trish isn't here. So neither does it matter that Trish gets up the noses of Gorman and Tate, his pub mates. Gorman is older and married, a tired good sport whose wife never shows up, even to fish him out. Tate is younger than Nick, and flash—not in fact as flash as Nick, but at the Cooper's Tate's reputation for superior flashness is a cornerstone of the social organization.

"How's Mrs. C?"

"Madame is away, boys."

"So soon? Recuperating, I'll wager."

"I'm recuperating. She goes from strength to strength."

"On the job?"

Gorman glares at Tate, holding to form.

"Do you mean, in the air?"

"Acrobatic bugger."

"Tate, you're pathological."

"Which reminds me: what ever happened to your posh one?"

"Johnny Colson. A friend, as you know."

"Then bring her round sometime. I'm sure the wife would get a kick out of that."

"Yes, by all means. You do that."

"She's in Canada at the moment, with her dad."

"Let it drift. Trust a married friend. The more they say they don't mind, the worse they feel. I'll lay odds that Trish lives in dread of your giraffe."

This thought is not new, but it pleases him. "Why do I . . . Someone get me another g&t."

THERE HAS ALWAYS BEEN A WOMAN, often unattained, holding his life in her hands. He is used to loving someone out of his league, mostly Johnny—too tall, too barmy, just beyond. Nick was always one of the hard lads at Spencer, the London school where his parents scrimped to keep him and his little brother William. But Nick's awe of skirt made him less hard than he looked.

With Trish you could take a leak without closing the door. He's never seen anyone as beautiful, including Johnny. He's never been with anyone as perfect, including the professionals. And she loves him totally, better or worse, marryingly. Even in the private moments, when he finds he can't breathe in her presence and blusters for fear of looking ridiculous, even then he can handle himself, because although she has the beauty she doesn't have the other thing, the beyond.

Johnny has treasured him like a good luck charm, a broken

lighter she refuses to chuck from her purse. Trish doesn't oper-
ate in a world of symbols. If she's too drunk to fuck, you can
fuck her. She likes you to get it in. She likes the taste of come.
She likes to taste herself on your dick, and she wants you to kiss
her, to taste it too.

She smiles at him in the morning as she's rolling the de-
odorant under her arms. It isn't even conscious. She likes Queen
and Roxette as much as the good stuff. She's up for anything on
the radio she can sing along to. When Trish gets old will she
have dry skin and sore subjects? He can't imagine. And of course
he will never give her reasons: he saw that show, growing up.

Trish has girlfriends, but not close friends. Nick isn't sure
how he feels about that. Men, after all, are considered bad with
secrets, but they're only bad with other people's secrets. Men
don't tell revealing things to anyone, and usually dislike having
to hear them. If a woman has a close friend she will tell her
everything, with no conception of danger. The entrusting of secrets is what defines a close friendship between women.

Nick thinks about Trish this way: he wonders if her lack of
confessors means she won't ever open up to him either. Or will
that trust be theirs to learn together over time? It's reassuring,
because women who are big on intimacy, and that's most of
them, always drill for more of it. But Trish won't try to barge into
him. When his door is closed, she won't knock, she'll wait. Still,
the enchanting ways in which she seeks contact—the smacks
and bites, conspiratorial giggles, private grooming—testify to
what's important: that she is present, has committed, and will
let her own door swing as wide as the hinges allow. Nick may not
open her essence the way he opens her legs, but at least he
knows that if it ever happens for her, it will happen with him.

TRISH HAS BOUGHT NICK a box of Havana cigars at the Duty Free and here in the taxi home she is deciding between the two cards she wrote on the plane. On one she's tried to be witty, but when she reads it back it doesn't seem to work. On the other, which she doodled for about an hour, she's written his name over and over, garlanded and wreathed in the pretty unoriginal style of teenage crushes, interposed with hearts bearing words like "forever," and "fuck me." This is way over the top. But it's how he makes her feel, so why shouldn't she show it?

Who am I kidding? He'll notice the cigars, not the girly note. No, really who am I kidding? He'll notice my bum. Like they always do.


NICK HAS STOPPED BY HARRODS after work to pick up smoked Scottish salmon, lemons, capers, brown bread, sweet butter and a bottle of Bollinger. He's cleaned the flat, had a bath and then cleaned that, put on fresh sheets and a Bryan Ferry CD. He hears the buzzer and opens the door. In a minute she's there, smiling but looking nervous.

"Must have a wee, must have a wash."

"How was it?"

"Oh, fine. I'm just tired, they were a lousy lot this time."

"I've organized a treat."

"Oh dear, really? I hate to disappoint. Do you mind if I just take a bowl of cereal and get in bed?"

"Of course not."

She watches a bad comedy on Channel Four with her knees

pulled up under the covers, but she doesn't look as if she feels at home. Nick isn't sure what to do but he can sense not to offer a shoulder rub or anything. He lies on his side next to her with his head propped up on one arm, watching the show. She feels lonely so he's lonely too.

"It doesn't seem real yet, does it?" Nick ventures.

She looks into his face, turning her head to align it with his.

"I guess not. Give it time, right?"

She reaches over, smiling, and knocks his propped arm out from under him. She pulls him near. They kiss, quick closed kisses on the lips. He waits for her to open her mouth but it doesn't happen. She slides under him and guides him in. He holds her waist, her calves, verifying rights. And now she kisses him, a proper hungry one. The fuck doesn't go on for long but it's good, and she doesn't let go after but rolls on top and grinds all of her onto him, gripping his thighs with her legs and ankles.

"Did you behave yourself, Mister?"

"Does wanking count?"

"Depends what you were picturing."

"Do I have to answer?"

"I'm your wife."

"I mustn't make you vain. You know how much I love you."

Trish smiles and pushes his hair from his face. "I've brought you a present from my travels."

"What is it?"

"You'll have to wait."

Trish hovers over his dick, brushing herself against him, smiling down, hooking her fingers into his mouth. When he's hard she fucks him again.

She goes to the kitchen to make tea. Nick lies in bed and

looks at the line of white sheet where it meets his belly. He isn't lonely now and he can imagine how there will be less and less of that for both of them.


IT'S AN AMBIVALENTLY SUNNY MONDAY MORNING. Nick calls Koestler, an atheist Jew he's known since school. Sarcastic and aloof, Koestler was not inclined to befriend potential assailants, which was how he viewed Nick, Nick's group, and certainly Tommy Stein-Ferguson, Nick's best friend. But Nick turned out to be funny and kind. Nick admired Koestler's tone with the masters—grave, correct, archly condescending. They built their friendship on music, drinking and their crushing lust for women.

"You've surfaced."

"Yes. Drinks today or tomorrow? Trish doesn't leave 'til Wednesday."

"Wednesday, then. I'm not ready to handle the sight of you married."

"I thought you hit it off?"

"I'd do her in a minute. So, Wednesday dinner."

"Who was that?" she shouts from the loo.

"Kess," he answers, wondering what it is about him Trish doesn't like.


EVEN WOMEN HE HAS LEFT BEHIND retain erotic power for Nick, glowing in the memory of an arm imprinted by the snug elastic of a blouse, a streak of house paint in untidy hair. It isn't the workings of the girl upon the world, but the workings of the world upon the girl that touch him. He must ask Kess for the literary history of this idea.

They meet at a Greek drinking club in Westbourne Grove. Downstairs, people dine on bad moussaka. Upstairs there are two rows of narrow tables, full of regulars drinking, shouting and smoking. They eat mezze with the oblivious fury of those who have come to drink and shout and smoke but are ambushed by the inspiration to shovel dishes of congealing taramasalata onto cold strips of pita toast. Nick arrives in the noise and smoke and amber lamps from a rainy night. Koestler is sitting with his back to the wall, halfway down the left side, triangulating a bowl of ice, a bottle of ouzo, and two glasses, one empty. Sitting opposite him in Nick's chair is Theo, the proprietor, an oddly phlegmatic and charmless man to preside over so social a business.

"Get out of my chair, you fat Greek bastard."

"Get out of my place, you nothing."

"Well said. Can I have a drink, please?"

"Ouzo good for you?"

"I need a cold lager first. What's the matter, Koestler?"

"Just watching a fellow immigrant stand up to John Bull."

Koestler sucks the ouzo off the ice in his glass and creates a fresh drink, spooning in cubes and adding the liquor carefully.

"How is your marriage?"

"Strange, but good. Not like living with a girl."

"You've never lived with a girl, Nick."

"I'm assuming. Not like having one to stay."

"For what it signifies."

"It's like being high the whole time in the way that everything is very specific. It's like looking out through a Viewmaster. The 3-D is so simple and extreme. And everything in the scene has been put there for a reason."

"It all means something."

"But you don't know what it is."

" 'Do you, Mister Jones?' And how does she feel about it?"

"She approaches it like a girl. She doesn't see things so much as she just feels them through her skin. But I know it's got to be a bit odd for her too."

"I'm sure you'll look back upon this time fondly. God help us."

IN A HOTEL ROOM NEAR THE FRANKFURT AIRPORT, Trish lies naked, face down on a heavy white duvet cover. She doesn't know the man with her, doesn't know why she let him buy her a drink at the hotel where they're both staying, doesn't know why she came to his room when the bar closed. She especially does not know why, when he kissed her in the bar, with his dark good-smelling skin, she didn't really resist. She liked his jokes, his soft voice, the way he seemed to fancy her enough but not too much. She was heading this way and he was heading that way. And there would be four days, two flights, and many showers be-tween him and home. He had fucked her quite well, eaten her out. She enjoyed watching the muscles on his shoulders while he did it. He has strong hands. What does that mean: strong hands? How is it measured? Breaking a golf ball, or lifting bags full of bricks? It's just a sexy idea, probably: hands that look like how men are supposed to be.

She lies on the cool linen and feels air over the small of her back. The man sits on the bed next to her, nicely, scratching her back. Is he a father? He begins using the tips of his fingers, not the nails, somewhere between chills and caresses, and applies almost enough pressure as the hand turns up from her bottom and in toward her spine for it to qualify as some kind of massage.

Now the hand goes down to her bum and the fingers spread out to widen the space, to make room for themselves. One finger ventures down to the front of her. As it pushes around she adjusts herself, moving her legs a little farther apart for him and freeing her tangled hairs.

It strolls along her oystery lips, dipping in and pulling out. Now it moves to the back, and just rests its weight against her, like she's the inkpad for his fingerprint. It turns a little to nestle in, sealing against her. Trish counts her heartbeats. The finger is moving again, capably, gathering her wetness and moving it back, reprinting, a little bit deeper and down and deeper still. After a few trips she feels it push into her. And out it goes again, gathering more of her wetness and bringing it back. The finger digs deeply until it is all the way in, two knuckles plus into her ass. Now it's fucking her, good finger, doing a good job. She feels good beneath it, and the finger seems happy too. Trish is moving with the rhythm and the feeling and the finger is a happy porpoise, corkscrewing in and stretching out, gracefully, too smoothly to disrupt the calm. Now a second finger joins the first, and two fingers are splashing in and out of her. Trish moves up against the good fingers and stretches, her arms and legs out in a long line.

Strange, but nice, and she knows from the man's breathing that he likes it a lot. Why? What's the fantasy? She breathes back: it isn't unconscious but not exactly a choice either, like when you just throw some fresh thyme into a stew you're making. Trish floats along, acting it out for this stranger. Because she knows he'll enjoy that, and because it's her contribution to the picnic. Suddenly she feels funny, self-conscious over her performance. On what plausible basis could he think she'd be coming from this? But her audience appears engrossed, unperturbed by a minor plot point.

In fact the nice man is thinking she is an anatomical anomaly or a dedicated actress. Either way, thank God the merciful.

She builds it and builds it, to make the moment work. His fingers plunge away. Now they're coming all the way out and she can feel the cool air of the room there, and now the sealing pressure again. She delivers her finale with a flourish of screams. Not a lie, just this person's fantasies projected back into him, which makes it kind of like she's the one doing the fucking. His dick is in his other hand, big and troubled. The fingers draw out of her and come to rest. Trish starts to roll over.

"You might want to get up carefully."

"Oh."

She pulls onto her knees, lifts herself off the bed, and darts to the bathroom. She looks back at herself in the mirror in the bright white light, and frowns. Her bottom is a finger painting. She stands in the bath, showers off, dries herself. She reappears, intending to suck him off, but the short wait has been too much. He sits in his come, looking young.

Trish smiles and dresses to go.

KOESTLER DOESN'T MIND if Nick isn't great company tonight. He can make the bar-chat, support his friend, and entertain himself by trying to work out what's going on in there. Not that Nick, in the firing line of new experience, has any idea himself. All Nick wants is to affirm that Koestler, and the antebellum truths he represents, will hold, that he can still pee on a favorite tree.

They talk politics as sports; sports as morality; morality as politics—the way men talk. They discuss tobacco. (It's one of their topics. Koestler and Nick can do half an hour on tobacco.) They do celebrity pussy.

Koestler likes Nick. They are friends, and Nick is a Jew, even if it's from the wrong side. Nick's father sold his culture, married an English girl, and sired the Clifford boys, pseudo-assimilated nothings without even a proper surname to go through life on. Koestler ventures his first exploration, needing to palpate the bruise in spite of himself.

"How did Grace and Marcus take to it all?"

Once, many years before, in the middle of what he said was a deal over rare coins, Marcus called Koestler and asked to borrow ten thousand pounds. He did it without telling Nick, but Nick found out. Koestler would not have hesitated to decline, despite Marcus' intimations that it could become a police matter, or worse. But it never came to that. Nick's apology was brief and painful, though not abject.

"I suppose they like her, not that they know her at all. She makes them nervous probably. But they're glad they can say I'm married, and that she's a nice girl, and polite, and of course really pretty."

"You aren't the most engaged of families, so that's a plus."

"That's always been a plus."

Nice legerdemain, you bastard, thinks Koestler. Not engaged, unless you count rage, disappointment, shame and silence—just normal life among the counterfeit goyim.


KOESTLER HAS A GRAY LINED RAINCOAT and a black waterproof fedora with some kind of plastic coating on the outside and flannel lining on the inside that really does the advertised job. He wears wool socks in his black lace-up boots. He loves the way he can walk across London in any weather with these perfected garments and remain truly warm and dry and comfortable. This is progress, science and the rag trade coming together to do clothes that really work. Koestler loves to walk and hates having to hold anything, above all an umbrella, while he does it. The coat has lots of clever inner pockets that close reliably so he can carry anything short of a pint of milk and still keep his hands free.

As always when he spends time with Nick, he leaves with feelings of fondness, and gratitude that he is Koestler and Nick is Nick. There are people he envies and people he pities, but no one else makes him so happy to be himself, so satisfied with the hand he's been dealt. Because Koestler at least knows how to play what he's holding.

The vacant taxis slow down on Baker Street, assuming he wants a ride. He can hear their diesels come up behind him, the comforting idle, the throat-clearing acceleration away. Koestler loves the sound. It is salvation renounced, salvation departing, salvation shrugging and going to find someone else to save. Schizophrenic Schadenfreude: joy at my other self's pain. Am I a masochist? Speak for yourself! *I'm* fine, but *you* keep hurting us! Koestler knows that his renunciations are only an act. He makes sure people think of him as stoic, glacial, unbuyable. So untrue: Koestler's every breathing moment is a sale. He sells himself with quiet joy, to every vice that will have him. It's just that many people's vices bore him: food, drugs, praise. He can't put reputation on the list because he works damn hard to sustain a reputation for not caring about what others think of him.

And Koestler loves the vices that are his own: solitude, tobacco, distant women, money above all. *Juden!* Though Koestler only loves money when it comes to him. Going to get it ruins the pleasure.

He turns around and in ten minutes is at the top of Queensway. He walks halfway down toward Kensington Gardens and into the Leipzigstube, a German restaurant that will be deserted at this hour. He orders a schnapps and a Warsteiner, then another schnapps. He loves the Leipzigstube as much as he loves Theo's. The place is dark and there are yellow paper napkins, folded in triangles. Koestler likes to drink, and is little affected by it. Sometimes he enjoys pushing himself into a steady silent drunkenness. He can go close to a week without sobering up, scrupulously modulating the buzz. He does it once or twice a year, usually but not always while abroad, a journey within a journey.

This, he knows, is not the start of such an arc, just a rainy London night when he's had a lot to drink. He takes the napkin from the place setting opposite him, and his own, and arranges them to form a Star of David. He pays his bill and leaves a big tip on the yellow star.

Outside, Koestler hails a taxi. He turns on the heater, thinking about women he's fucked. And to the maternal throb of the diesel, he falls asleep for the ride home.


TRISH HAS NO ONE NOT TO TELL about her encounter and little time, except for a few minutes during flights, to think about Frankfurt. She sits with her legs crossed, parallel from the knees down, twisted a little to one side on the center aisle seat in Business Class. It's like this whenever she's had her bum played with: she feels vaguely brainless for half a day or so, as if her short-term memory lived up there somewhere. Sitting down is worse because it feels like something's coming out of her, even though she knows it isn't. At least the seatbelt light means she can close her eyes and spare herself chatting up the clients.

She thinks about marriage: the word, herself as a married woman. Is it what she expected? Has she ever expected anything in particular? She always figured she would be, always assumed that among the men who sniffed her out there would be one sweet enough, cute enough, enough of a laugh. Nick was it, from almost the first look. Good to have and better to hold, as she read once in a magazine.

A magazine article is what it's been like, or an American film. Nick is straightforward that way. He's handsome. Not fall-down handsome, except for the clear green eyes that make him look like a friendly fox. He's decent and honest. Clever too, with clever friends to prove it. Trish is a girl who grew up protecting her dad and wanting to be nothing like her mum, so how perfect she'd pick a boy who loves his mum and got let down by his dad every time he tried to believe in him.

She can't explain why, but it makes some kind of bond between them. Trish takes pride in being a useful girl, capable, agile and self-contained. She dwells so little on sorrowful thoughts that she almost forgets she has them. But there's a part of her, a young place, tender to the infrequent touch. And Nick touches it without even meaning to, again and again, and makes it better.

What happened, in this second week of her marriage—does she feel bad about it? How can she? It has no connection to her real life. From the taxi away to the taxi home, it's as if she's perpetually airborne, at an alternate altitude. What did Admiral Nelson say? Every man is a bachelor past Gibraltar. She can no more regret it than regret a dream, which is sort of what it was—except that with a dream she doesn't feel her heartbeat in her bottom the next morning. Maybe one day it won't occur to her to do such a thing, or maybe this time it happened because it didn't yet occur to her not to. Not like Mum's fucking around. That was no accident—it was the active theater in the family war.

Trish loves her mother but not how she behaves. Mum is generous, easy, easily impressed. She was pretty and she still is. Mum believes that healthy girls get carried away. She'd be proud of Trish and her independence. A little secret spice to keep things fresh. But contemplating her mother's approval has almost got Trish regretting last night. She likes men. She's a curious girl. And it's how you find out about them, you take their willies out.

That's how it happened with Nick. Now they share a flat. They'll buy things together, dine out, go on trips. They'll grow old together. Nick is more than sweet. Nick is super-sweet. She gets to turn him on, secure in knowing she will always turn him on, totally.

And then there's the other thing, the touching the secret place thing. It isn't what she means when she tells people on the phone how she's fallen in love. It's something else, something that could take time, but it might be what falling in love really is.

She sees from her parents' example how some people just fuck around on each other to make their lives miserable, and that will never happen because Nick will never know about it. If you aren't out to hurt people, they needn't get hurt. It's easy to be careful if you are full of care and not just playing a game with yourself. She has to be honest about it because she doesn't want to make a mistake. She won't lie to herself, like Mum, not know-ing her own mind. Something like last night happens out of his-tory. She dreamt it. This tree won't make a sound when it falls in the forest.

But what if she's wrong and it could be a problem? Then it won't happen again. It's like a pub you stop going to when you move to a different tube stop. And what if it makes her sad? That's another reason for it not to happen again. Not like a de-cision, she just knows herself. She'd never choose a tricky feel-ing over a simple one. There is temptation—every unseen cock is a temptation to some degree—but temptation is not her prob-lem. She isn't resisting, it's just a certain "I think not" kind of clarity.

She'll know the instant she walks through the door of the flat. If she even remembers to ask herself, then the answer is never again.

IT'S SATURDAY AFTERNOON when Trish returns from Heathrow. Nick is out playing squash, but he's left a note, a big bunch of daisies in a vase, and a good bar of bittersweet chocolate by the side of the tub. She's in the bath, eating her chocolate and scan-ning a copy of *Hello*, when Nick comes through the front door and through the bathroom door. There isn't much left on him to get wet as he climbs into the tub over her.

"Aren't you a poppet, leaving me flowers and sweets! Will I always get this treatment?"

"Yes, you will."

She puts an arm around him and an arm under.

"Give it over. I'm sure it needs a good wash."

He's hard in her hand. She puts him in her mouth. Nick is curious.

"First I'm going to jerk you off right here, because I want a good slow fucking."

The chocolate taste of her mouth, the wetness, the warmth of her winter lips are as much around him as the small strong hand that knows what to do with his business. He shoots off operatically, from the diaphragm. Trish drags him to the bed to put him to further use.

"SHALL WE STAY IN or go out?" asks Nick.

"Oh, out, please. I'm feeling festive."

"Tommy's got a dinner party going with Belinda, and then everyone's off to the Clermont. Would you like us to join?"

Tommy Stein-Ferguson is Nick's true friend. Everything else he can't help. He's big, over six foot two, and fleshy in a red-cheeked way. His hair is of a blackness and heft that women not only fancy, they envy. His sea-blue eyes, long lashes and straight nose are out of a fairy tale. Tommy wasn't a clever boy, but a casual cruelty added to his appeal. He also belched, farted, gobbed and snotted, which should have made him repellent. But women found everything about him adorable. As Tommy grew up, unexpected things happened: he got wiser and kinder and somewhat better mannered, but no less handsome. Somehow the bogus yearning quality he had mastered in youth, to beguile the earnest and elder, had become real, like crossed eyes you were warned would stick.

Nick knows Trish fancies Tommy. Of course she does. You can tell the DNA to shut up, but you can't change its mind. No matter, because Tommy won't ever touch her, out of loyalty to his friend. And though Trish may not grasp it, Diana Stein-Ferguson would never squander his beauty on a Saloon Bar tart. Not even one, miraculous heir to generations of carbolic soap and coal dust, with skin as perfect as her son's.

Tommy will be a godfather to Nick's child, and Nick to Tommy's, so family events will put Trish and Tommy in rooms together. The men see each other all the time, for football, or meals, or things at the Stein-Fergusons'. Nick has been a fixture there since boyhood, like a character in some English novel he knows he should have read. That won't be the case much any more, now that Trish is around. It pleases him to know that Diana admires his discretion in such matters. The way opens and the way closes again, whether or not one sees it at the time. This is as near as Trish will get to their sort of people. Nick hopes she learns early and doesn't fret over it.

Trish is never at ease with Tommy's friends, and particularly not with Belinda. She has been so unfailingly nice that Trish wants to flatten her, though Belinda can't tell. She's just thick enough that her niceness may be genuine. Trish met girls like her at art college. Trish's family wasn't posh but Dad had made a bit, and good things—cars, clothes, school in the country—got spent for, for his girl.

Belinda is tall, athletic and up for fun—belching away with Tommy, scaling parapets, doing a few lines for a laugh. But she is fundamentally sensible, ostentatiously sound. Being more re-strained than him is something Tommy likes in a girl. So his wilder pranks—thievery, totaling cars—are not Belinda's line of country. She laughs and scolds and cooks her cookery-course dinner party dinners just like a wife, which, although Tommy knows better, she may become. By impulse and good sense,

90 percent of the time, Trish would have said let's meet them after dinner at the club. But she's feeling fine, and fuck-all confident.

"Oh, in for a penny."

Tommy lives in the downstairs floors of a house in Langton Street. There are ten people around the table in a smallish dining room. Belinda organizes trivets and dishes, looking capable. The food—some fish in a white-wine sauce, duck in green and pink peppercorns with lentils and oiled potatoes, a salad with cheese on it, and berries with mascarpone—is impressive for its punctuality, not its flavor. Nothing is quite right. Not noticeably overcooked or undercooked, but did anyone sample it during preparation? Tommy's got good wine to go with each course. Everyone drinks a lot and speaks loudly and interrupts each other to confirm a state of levity. Trish admires Belinda's production while enjoying the knowledge that anything she makes would taste better.

It comes up that one of the girls' mothers had been a stewardess with BEA in the fifties—flew Comets to Malta or something. "Right, Trish, didn't you used to . . . ?" The dreaded topic has arisen, and yes, she did, before transitioning to the marketing job. But it's OK, just the Home Counties' idea of good fun for a girl back when there was a BEA to fly. Like marketing, today. So Trish laughs too.

There are phone calls to radio cabs and bottles of Bollinger for the road. The section caravans to Berkeley Square. An obsequious greeting for the boisterous toffs, then blackjack for the men, roulette and piss-taking for the girls. Cornering an area, cognacs, restlessness, the Vanessa or Del's argument. Del's wins, more fuss and coats and taxis over from Mayfair. Down the stairs, flopping down at a long table. Finally, stumbling into the lights, Trish drags Nick onto the little dance floor. The DJ cuts out of something new and into "Got to Be Real," from the seventies.

Trish dances well, with lots of eye contact—like she fucks, of course. She puts Nick's hands on her hips and smiles at him in the way that he's dreamt of someone doing since he was a boy. The song changes to "Brick House," the dancers move from the two to the one. Trish goes with it in a charming, married way. Only in the eyes and the pleasured pout is Nick given his private signal that she loves to be his.

Around four-thirty they all cross Portman Square to the business hotel for a fried breakfast, smoking a pair of fat joints to transition the curling edge of tiredness into an impression of appetite. Tommy eats and then snores on Belinda's shoulder: the two things look different but sound about the same. Nick listens to a broker boy's view on interest rates, gamely but with scant attention. Belinda's baby sister Claudia—shorter, but more of a catch—assesses the state of modern portrait painting to a fellow calculating his endgame to get her home with him.

Trish looks around the restaurant packed with bleary revelers: a cross-section of well-born and just rich people, domestic and imported, young and youngish. With different choices, it strikes her, she could be sitting at more than half of these other tables, her life connected to these other people's lives. All she cares about is that Nick should be the one by her side, the one she is going home with, the one who is her own. Only Nick's lap will do for the taxi ride home. So that the whole purpose of the evening has been to propel events in order to make certain that this coming moment would occur. The restaurant billows before her sleepy eyes like a special effect from some sixties film. She tugs on his belt loop. They rise, speak, smile and depart, her arm around his waist, and emerge into the indeterminate light of the taxi queue. There's definitely some spring in the air.


SUNDAY A WEEK LATER Nick is playing football with a bunch of old school friends, bankers, traders and some of Tommy's brother's set. The match is near Oxford. Tommy has given Nick a lift out the night before, so Trish, to her regret, has agreed to ride with Koestler. He shows up in an Aston Martin borrowed from Fitz, who wants it to drive back in. Koestler and Fitz are friends from university. Fitz is friends with Twelve, who knew Tommy in prep school. Twelve's family owns the pile where the match and the weekend are happening. Twelve is a presumptive term since Eleven, minus a prostate and most of his senses, remains confirmedly among the living.

"Would you like to drive the beast?" asks Koestler, with suspect sunniness.

"Oh my God, what is it?"

"It's a touring car, I believe. I warn you, I'm a terrible driver."

It's true. Koestler is pushy and slow to react, and he shows minimal concentration. Trish gets the impression that Koestler wouldn't mind the thing crashing, were he not in it. Trish is a good driver, and on the M40 she wonders how to suggest a change of seats. Koestler is showing off his inability, practically playing bumper cars.

"You're a terrible driver, as you said."

"Well I warned you."

"Can we switch over? Nick would never forgive me for letting you kill us."

"I think he'd forgive you for killing me, actually."

She won't ask again because she can tell it's just more power for him to feel high on. Maybe engaging a conversation will take the edge off this exhibition.

"You two are a funny pair to be friends."

"Meaning you don't like me."

"It's strange that you're friends. What does he see in you?"

"Well there's history—school history no less. There's that. Do you know what I see in Nick? I'm drawn to his goodness, the same as you. I'm good too, Trish, despite what I know you think"—he pronounces her name like a brand of washing-up liquid—"but I need to make an effort. My instincts, my first thoughts, are for myself. Not even what's good for me, just what would be amusing at any given moment. Still, I do try. I like to be good. I like the picture of it. I cultivate a style of goodness."

"Not so as anyone would notice."

"No, you're right. I'm a failure at appearing to be good. But just as I am much better than my instinct would have me be, I am also much better than I show. I almost invariably behave well."

"But people still see you for what you are."

"Oh dear. What am I?"

The car has slowed by at least twenty miles per hour and Koestler, who can't fence and change lanes at the same time, is keeping to the left, although with a tendency to drift toward the median.

Koestler continues, "People, women especially, generally see one for whom one is."

"Then it really is big of you to make the effort. Since there's no credit in it."

"None, none at all. And it's like that with my sexual energy. Women tend to fear it, however much I try to play it down."

"You are such a rodent!"

"Oh, you're misunderstanding me. I don't flatter myself. I'm not saying it's attractive. Just the opposite, as we both know. Women either like me or they don't, and usually they don't. But they all assume I want to jump on them."

"We do?"

"The ones I want to jump do. However I handle myself, it seems they can always tell."

This would be a good time to redirect the conversation. "So what did you and Nick get up to at school?"

"We didn't get up to much. Different friends. He was sporty and I was a swot."

"You were?"

"I was, though I always kept my hard work to myself. And I didn't have very many friends, as you can imagine. But Nick didn't judge me, and for that reason I did not judge him. Then we started hanging around on weekends, going down to the pub, chasing the same girls."

"Who won?"

"Neither of us. The girls, usually. So we'd drink and commiserate. Just a couple of young losers, talking about popular music."

"And after you left school?" Trish wants to stretch the conversation and smooth it out, make it work on Koestler's driving for as long as she can.

"After school it got easier. But you need to add in the Johnny factor." Koestler tries to read her response. "Nick's friend Johnny Colson. Have you met her yet?"

"No, I've only heard about her."

"She's OK. Mad as a Spaniard, which I think she is, way

back somewhere. A lovely girl with blue eyes and Pre-Raphaelite hair. But that Spanish Catholic blood is in there, and it makes her crazy."

"Did you go out with her too?"

"Too? Neither one of us went out with her."

That's new information. Trish hasn't probed about the friendship, but an unrequited love is more of a bother than one that's been fed. Koestler senses her reaction and Trish knows it.

"Nick was mad for her, but he was over it before you ever came on the scene." They are reassuring words, meant to not re-assure. "Even he came to realize she's too freaked to fuck with."

"And you and she are friends too?"

"I can't say that. I know her. I'm fond of her. We know each other through Nick and through Johnny's friend Lucy. But she's really rather a stupid girl. I'm not being mean, just accurate. You, for example, are smart. She isn't. That's just the truth."

They watch the road ahead of them darkening. Koestler thinks of playing with the car again but decides to play with Trish some more instead.

"The one I'm devoted to is Lucy. She is smart, and not fucked up. Or a lot less fucked up anyway. I would drop any-thing to polish Lucy's silver or take her cat to the vet. But Lucy with me is like Johnny with Nick. We are men who were con-sidered and rejected."

"I bet you had spots."

"A few. No scars, you'll notice. But we all feel bad about our burdens, don't we?"

"What was the matter with Johnny?"

Trish is more eager to obtain information, even tainted, than to maintain her leverage with this little shit. Koestler can hear it in her voice, and feel it in the magnetic fields around the body next to him. It's the familiar combination. Cruel dismissal, but still the scent of prey: his usual poison.

"Johnny, as I said, is a mixed-up kid. Daddy issues—a handsome, destructive bastard. Never touched her, I'm sure, but he made sure she dreamt about it. So Johnny gets the double: the psychic wound and the guilt for it on top. Mum's pretty, one of those self-damaging numbers. You can figure all the ways she did that—all the ways you can. So Johnny has a screwy home, a screwy life. She's just a screwy girl with very long legs. And as I said, she was mad to begin with, like the parents, from the genes. And because she is dim, per Mama, there isn't much hope of her figuring it out."

Trish doesn't speak but Koestler still hears the question.

"Nick wouldn't tell you anything different. He wouldn't say what I have said, but he wouldn't disagree with the facts. Poor Nick. He wanted to save Bambi but Bambi didn't want to be saved. The bite of the trap is the only feeling she can trust."

"You're like the Marks & Sparks knock-off of a Bond villain. So arrogant behind the wheel of your rich friend's motor car."

"Patricia. Going for the anti-Semitic remark just tells us you're rattled. Well, you're true to your class. And that's the real problem here. Nick loves you, no question. But you're a bit of a consolation prize. And very consoling too, I don't doubt. Here's a thought: why don't I pull over so you can suck my dick? Really, I think we should. Those beautiful eyes should be looking up over a full mouth."

Hating Koestler is pointless, he does the job well enough himself. But she can't bear that Nick sees no more clearly than to have him for a friend. The presence of such a person can curse lives.

"Now why did I say that? Oh, because you might have said

yes. I don't see excessive self-esteem as being one of your challenges in life. It would have made me happy. But more than that, it would have made you sad. Hey, I'm only testing you—your sense of humor if you're bright, or your loyalty if you're thick."

She's boiling.

"No, fair enough. We both know I mean it. Here's the thing. Nick and I have been friends a long time. He knows me. And I'm certainly not the one he's afraid of here. That's how we stay friends. Because however black my soul, I have no power to harm him. You know what the Arabs say? That a husband should beat his wife every night, because he may not know why she deserves it, but *she* does."

Trish hates him, and she hates his driving. Now she isn't even sure what he's trying to say. Koestler seems to know exactly where he's taking this. But he stops talking and drives on, moderately. She could take complete control of this worm, if she wished, and he would let her, lose his mind to her, for the pleasure of watching her fall. It must always end like this, she thinks. When it's time for the kill he turns the knife on himself.

THEY ARRIVE AT TWELVE'S PLACE just before nightfall, a Sunday in the country at the trailing end of winter. There are cars in the gravel and on the lawns, clothes and people and bottles strewn everywhere. In the house it's just as chaotic. People are going in and out of rooms, getting in and out of baths. Muddy men, newly clean men, laughing women, short-tempered women. The texture of the weekend has worn through to this, and no one is bothering with manners any more, no one is closing doors. The seated dinner has been scratched in favor of conversations in the stairwell, passing bottles of good claret, smoking cigarettes with ashtrays in hand; in favor of sixteen conflicting projects in the kitchen, mostly involving the toasting of bread and melting of cheese and scrambling of eggs. The servants poke heads in to assess the bomb site that will be left for them. People will leave now, people will leave late, people will leave first thing tomorrow. People will announce one plan, and then another, and do something else again.

Into this rip tide of rich faded youth turn Koestler, in one direction, and Trish, in another. Koestler finds Fitz, hands over the car keys and hears the plot. Something a bit destructive is called for. An injurious poker game? An injurious night of drugs? Gun play? Trish, a deportee who has yet to lose her papers or her dignity, wanders with her satchel in search of Nick. After scanning the scenes through several doorways, Trish finds the room she's looking for. Nick is bathed and dressed, lying on a double bed, reading the "How to Spend It" pages of the *Financial Times*, listening to Frank Sinatra—one of the Nelson Riddle albums—on a boom box.

"Darling!"

He looks up and sees Trish. He puts down the paper and opens his arms. She climbs onto the high bed next to him.

"Got any fags?"

Nick's got a box of Marlboro Mediums. He lights one for her.

"Did you win?"

"No, we lost. It was seven–two, or maybe six–two. We never worked it out. And I'm hurt."

"Oh, my poor thing."

"How was the drive?"

"Nothing to report."

"Hungry?"

"Famished."

"We'll have to go fight for our supper. Society is breaking down around here."

"So who did you sleep with last night, Mr. Clifford?"

"I was spoiled for choice. So in the end it was just me and my radio."

"Saving all your love for me?"

"Most of it, certainly."

"Shall we venture down into the madness?" Trish wouldn't mind a look around the savage luxury, familiar to her only from BBC dramas, as long as Nick is there by her side.

"At your pleasure, ma'am."

"Good. And then let's go back to town. You've got work tomorrow."

"You've only just driven up."

"Oh, I don't care about that. But can we take the train back? So we don't have to be chatty with anyone."

Trish doesn't want any more close combat with Nick's tricky friends, just her man by her side, a bite, a blur of life, and maybe a quick crack at Twelve's cellar.

The whole party is more tired than it knows—by ten the ones left are planning their routes home. As their taxi pulls out, Trish sees the Aston Martin parked where they'd left it. She hasn't seen Koestler since they came in. Why does she care? Is it just to reassure herself that he won't turn up at their compartment, like in a bad film? She wants to spend the train ride alone with Nick, not watching him talk smart with this awful person.

She must have slept on the train, she thinks, the trip was so fast. She spent it as she had hoped, with "What's Going On" leaking out of Nick's headphones and her hand inside his shirt, resting on his belly.

It's almost one when they get to Paddington. Unbending stiff limbs and scooping up bags, they walk wordlessly through the quiet station. An interval of funny feeling, as they are each struck by how new they are, how little they really know each other, and how much they are going to learn.

THE VOICE IS ALWAYS ADRENAL for him. Often, because it comes at odd hours, it finds him asleep, or in a mood, or in an awkward place to talk. It's smooth and musical. The syntax and tone are finely pitched, but he can always tell how nuts she is from the first few syllables. This time it's about an eight. Nick has just come off the floor for a bite of lunch. It's been a hectic session, good fun. Trish flew out this morning, Tuesday, and will be back Saturday late. He notes that his second thought, after recognizing the voice, is to his wife's whereabouts.

"Is that you, Nick? You sound different."

"It's me, Johnny. I'm just a bit hoarse from my morning yell."

"What's the share *du jour*?"

"Everybody's shorting today."

"And you? Are you shorting?"

"With everything I'm made of. Where are you?"

"I'm back in town. Can we get a drink?"

"Five-thirty at the Savoy?"

"I'll be there. Father?"

"Yes, my child?"

"Is it true?"

"Yes it is."

"Four-thirty at the Savoy."

"Five-thirty."

"That's what I meant."

After the close he gets a taxi, despite the rain. Nick sees Johnny before she sees him. She's been there for a while, not drinking, just nursing her first g&t but probably down half a pack of smokes. The sight of her has a power over him still, but what that power is now he can't quite summon.

"Colson."

"Hey there!"

She stands up, five ten and nine stone of honey blond.

"You're married!"

"This is true."

"My God. And?"

"I met this girl."

"Trish?"

"Yes, Patricia Anne Taylor. Trish. What can I say? Apparently she's always been 'Trish.' I met her a few months back. Actually, I met her first about a year ago, upstairs at Harvey Nichols. But that night we were sailing under different flags. Then I saw her again in January, at breakfast in the Fulham Road. I remembered her, remembered her name, I went right for it. We've sort of been together since."

"What's she like?"

"She's sweet. Lots of fun. Very can-do, like a girl in an adventure novel."

"I hear she's a beauty."

"She is."

Nick brings out his wallet, motioning to a waiter for two more gin and tonics. He hands her three photographs, takes a green olive and sucks on it.

"Oh my, yes. Nice smile, great tits, small, just the way you like them. Great legs! This must keep you in at night."

"When she's around. She travels for work."

"International marketing guru, right?"

"Relocation Marketing, for the Emirates. It means touring UK and European suits around the Gulf, helping the sheiks show off development opportunities. Translation: give them a good time. She's gone about every other week."

"And how is that?"

"It's OK for now, it means I get some work done. And it makes the change a bit more gradual. But I definitely feel married."

"I should have plucked you when I had the chance."

"Things worked out for the best."

"What will you do?" It comes out sounding desperate.

"I've done it. Now we live our lives. One day she'll stop traveling. We'll have kids, argue over what kind of car we can afford. She'll be the sensible one."

"Is it nice?"

Nick takes her hands from the Benson & Hedges pack and holds them in his. The palms are damp.

"It's nice. We make toast. We make love. We make plans, but mostly just for the weekend."

Nick reads her for a moment.

"I know what you're asking me, and why. Yes, it is possible to be happy. I'm mad about this girl and also I am happy. The two things can go together, it turns out. But it still doesn't feel entirely real. I look at her face sometimes, like when she's reading or watching the telly. I look at her nose, the shape of her ears, the incredible line of her jaw. And it makes me so happy, but also confused. Is this really all for me? What possessed her?"

"She likes you. Have you thought about me?"

Nick watches Johnny twirl a ring of hair. He really hasn't thought about her much.

"Of course. I've been in love with you for a long time. It's the feeling that I compare all others to."

Johnny lights a cigarette and watches the flame as she does it, to ask the next question.

Nick replies, "I've dreamt of this meeting, all the times when I felt sick from wanting you. But all I've got is love. Nothing else. Things won't be how I wanted, but I don't want those things any more. It's just that it can't be how it was, with me always ready to come to you. You know?"

"Of course, yes."

"But we can be close."

"Just different?"

"Yes. Am I saying this? I used to think of your kiss."

"We've kissed."

"Yes, but the taste was given under different terms than it was received."

"I remember what you taste like. I like what you taste like."

"I believe you. But it was different. You've felt my desire and forgiven it, because you know that even when I comfort you, I'm still a man—and not the man for you. You might have given me my dreams, I know, but only out of tenderness, not out of hunger like I was feeling. Love makes everything different."

"It makes you different." She says it with fondness.

"I love how it is, so I can't miss how it was. You're such a good soul. You'd never claim something that you don't want. And what you do want is what you will always have. What am I saying here? Is it clear?"

"You can't conceive how happy I am, really. But it's a shock, you know? Perhaps we shouldn't see each other. Maybe it's too hard for me."

"That's up to you."

"Do you have plans tonight?"

"Trish is away until Saturday."

The rain has stopped. They walk up into Covent Garden, head west, cross Shaftesbury Avenue into Soho, cross Soho, then Regent's Street into Mayfair. Walking is one of the natural states of their friendship. Mostly Johnny talks, about Canada, her mother, her brother—rarely her sister or her father. She talks about a man she had been seeing, a man she is seeing now, her father's latest woman. Nick admits to himself that it's all less interesting when you aren't hung up on fucking her, or rather not fucking her. Johnny plans to be around, in town and in the country, for a few months. Trish will want to meet her. He knows Johnny does not want to meet Trish but he will need to arrange it, once at least.

The charm of Johnny is never the text of what's happening but the notes scribbled in the margins. It's the rhythm of how they walk together, the telepathy by which they choose what street to take, the looking into shops and moving on at the same moment. Nick loves her generous spirit, the way she can be insightful even while she is always seeking the best in people. It takes more than his desire and her comfort to make them spend ten, fifteen, twenty hours alone together and want to do it again the next day. Their minds are well shaped to each other after so much time. It's a different energy than there will ever be with Trish, one more fitting a friend than a wife.

They find themselves outside Tamarind and go in, hungry. They eat too much because they have to have some of a lot of things and then more of the ones they love. Full of Kingfisher and cardamom, they get a taxi back to Johnny's sister's house in Campden Hill Square. The sister and her husband are giving a dinner party; they pass through it, greeting but declining to join. They go to the big sitting room in the basement, the Moroccan one that isn't for formal company, and sprawl on the cushions with an ashtray and a bottle of Calvados. Johnny scampers upstairs and back down, holding a fistful of Havanas for Nick, grinning. It's all fine again.

Nick gets home after three, forwarding through the machine to the message he wants: "It's me, darling. It's late and I'm going to sleep. Do leave a little cream for your pussy. I love you. Sweet dreams."


JOHNNY DOUBLE-LATCHES THE FRONT DOOR and goes to her bedroom on the fourth floor. She takes her clothes off, puts on a tee shirt (*Scorpions Live in Moscow*, liberated from her brother), and takes her station in front of the sink. She brushes her teeth for two minutes, using first a fluoride toothpaste and then Euthymol. She washes her face with something called a rectifying bar, for about a minute and a half. She studies her cheek and finds two barely visible blackheads, which she extrudes into a tissue. She treats the tiny exit wounds with witch hazel. She massages Belgian moisturizer into her face, and one made in Spain onto her hands and elbows, heels and knees. She gets in bed with the remote. Passing the soft porn and Nordic dance music videos, she finds an old American sitcom, dubbed into German. It's about a pig-faced boy who, encouraged by his widowed father, keeps a pet bear. Johnny turns out the light and puts her thumb in her mouth to watch.

TRISH IS ON THE TOILET. It's Sunday morning. Nick walks in and finds her hands between her legs. Trish looks up, startled to see him awake. She stares at Nick, waiting for a reaction. Nick isn't putting it together. Trish motions for him to kneel in front of her.

"It's a science project."

She puts the white plastic strip on the sink and reaches for some toilet paper. A few drops of pee glisten on her soft hairs like Christmas ornaments. Nick looks up at her and she looks down at him.

"I love you."

"I love you."

Nick reaches around Trish's legs and slides her forward. He sticks his tongue out, touching just under one of the ornaments, and it breaks onto his tongue. He does another and then another. He slides her farther forward and parts her legs to open her up. He burrows in and finds the other wet that is there for him. Her legs are over his back. She holds on to the wall and the side of the sink, her feet pointing off into space. Nick watches her happy frown as she grips the sink and the towel bar to position herself against his dedicated mouth. They mash into each other when she comes, focused on the waves of energy that roll from her center out to her fingers and toes and the roots of her hair, until everything grows calm.

"Is it time?"

"Let's look."

Two blue stripes cross the plastic tab, flying like a sailboat's ensign in a Renoir painting Nick once saw.

"I'll check with my doctor."

"But it looks like?"

"It looks like yes."

LIFE IS DIFFERENT AFTER THE NEWS. The office transfers Trish to a town job, normal hours and no travel. She stops drinking and smoking and tries to eat healthy food. Nick cooks for her or takes her out for big meals at unfamiliar restaurants. Trish wants to eat all sorts of things, like in the books. Her biggest craving— not the best idea, but she's being so good every other way that it doesn't occur to them—is for oysters. Two or three times a week they meet in the evening at Scott's for icy trays of raw Belons. Nick doctors his with sea salt and horseradish and peppers. Trish eats hers—a dozen at a sitting—neat from the shell, sucking down the liquor. Nick urges her to sniff the oyster before she eats it, but Trish thinks it's poor manners.

"But you can get a bad one anywhere. If it doesn't smell right, pass."

So Trish sniffs, giggles and slurps. They seem to be laughing all the time, and hugging and fucking.

Trish comes to meet Nick at the Exchange over lunch. She drags him into the Ladies' Lounge, pulls him into a stall, and spreads her hands against the wall, turning her head back to snog him. Nick lifts up her dress.

"You aren't wearing any."

He buries his face in her.

"Come on, man!"

Nick stands up to get his penis out. Trish reaches back to guide it.

"Push it in."

It goes a little way and Nick rocks it sideways against her.

Trish's hand keeps him on course as the shaft picks up her slick-ness. He fucks her with slow shudders. Then holds on inside her and leans back, to watch her twitching jewel as she gets hers. He pulls out, still sore with lust. Trish turns around, sits on the loo, and sucks him soft and clean.

"Kiss me."

Nick is flushed, he has a fever, he is flustered and he wants more.

"Wait!"

They hear the door shut as someone leaves the bathroom.

"Now!"

They dash out like kids playing pirate.

NICK IS ON THE TUBE heading to work. He is aswirl with joy, but too full of it to feel it as joy. He loves this woman, easily to death and past it. She has his child in her body. The future is an in-visible city but the road to it is wide and tree-lined. His face is hot. Suddenly he is afraid that he is going to cry. He gets out at the next stop, climbs the escalator as quickly as he can, and sur-faces about a mile from the Exchange. As he walks through the rainy morning his tears come, first running down his face, then with big sobs he can't control. "I'm gonna go outside . . . in the rain." The Dramatics, was it Buddah Records? His whole life he has wondered what this would be like, and here he is. He wants to run but he walks carefully. *I have people to protect.*

TRISH AND NICK SPEND THE WEEKENDS looking for a new flat. They find two bright floors with a small garden in Kentish Town. Kitchen and sitting room on the ground floor, bedrooms and a bath on the first. For thirty-six hours they angle with brokers, hoping their offer will be accepted. The news comes on a joyous Sunday evening.

They make lists, take stock of what they have, what they need to buy, what will and won't do. They visit the OB, and see a gray image of something small and precious moving inside of Trish. In the center of it a dot flickers as fast as a strobe—the heart, they are told. Trish says the baby looks like Nick. He says it looks like a Beatrix Potter rabbit. At this stage, they laugh, it could be either.

The flat in West Hampstead no longer feels like home. It's a staging area for the life to come. Things are going into boxes and the boxes are going into separate corners. Other things arrive and go directly into the Kentish Town corner, admired but un-opened. By the beginning of the second trimester they have started telling their friends and families. Everyone is bathed in their glow, and glows back. Everyone throws a party. It seems as if Trish and Nick spend less time together alone, even though they spend more, because there are always plans to make, deci-sions, discussions. There is always a topic to address. When they cuddle, when they fuck, when they curl up and Nick sings into Trish's rounding, hardening belly, the time feels stolen from present needs, as delicious as an affair. Nick's mood evens, but there's wild joy residing just below the surface.

IT'S TWENTY OF TWO on a clear summer day. Trish is at the office in Bond Street. She's looking out the window because she's thinking about lunch, and that's why she sees him coming from the left on the other side of the street and crossing over diago-nally toward her. He is handsome, of standard size and coloring, with a lizardy grace. He looks pleased with himself, like a Jesuit. The man's name is Joe Somerville. Trish was with him for six years, from a time when she was very young. Joe went to university and then magazines, and then to something else. He's done well, but after a few single malts he'll explain how he's blown through his intellectual capital. Joe has a Jaguar and an expensive flat on the South Bank and a habit of buying and selling country houses, because he's never happy with what he's got or where he's got it. He's smart and industrious and unconflicted about the big stuff, which for Joe means his place in the world. He likes making money and traveling. He likes pretty girls. He likes his good clothes, although he doesn't care about them. He heard the news about Trish, and that's when he decided that she was what he really wanted.

Trish knows he is there by no accident. The call comes from Reception. She reviews herself quickly and goes to meet him.

"Hello, Patricia. You look amazing. Had lunch yet?"

"Joe. How are you?"

"I'm extremely well, but you're even better. I mean, my God!"

"Thanks. There's a lot that's happened."

"And I want to know all about it—that's why I'm here. We must celebrate."

"I'm a bit swamped."

"That's OK. Delighted to wait."

With the cute smile, Joe moves to a low table where the brochures are. He puts on his reading glasses, a flattering addition since Trish's day. They remind her of those photo shoots of James Dean, being studious in borrowed black spectacles. Banking, infrastructure, family fun. Trish doesn't look at Nadia, the receptionist, who pretty much figures what's going on.

At two Trish reappears, taking Joe's arm in a form of counter-attack. They walk to the Westbury. Joe asks about her life and Trish answers and Joe smiles. As Trish is telling her story, she is struck by its believability. But every hair on her body is charged to Joe's presence. Every move he makes affects her, as if the space between them were filled with some connective fluid. At the hotel, the Garden Room is mostly empty. Joe orders champagne, which Trish doesn't touch after Joe's toast. Joe drinks as he solicits more details of her life. They eat smoked trout. Joe doesn't mention the history, which only makes it more present.

"I know I can't keep you. You've got to get back. But it's silly we aren't pals, isn't it?"

"No, I think it's completely sensible."

"This was too short."

"This was nice, but I'm afraid I have to go."

A sudden desolate look passes across Joe's face. Trish knows the act but is not immune to it. Joe's face snaps back. He leaps up and comes around to pull out Trish's chair. He rests a light hand upon her shoulder.

"It was lovely to see you."

He leans around and kisses her cheek.

"Bye, Joe."

She stands and makes it out the door and onto the street. She is bursting with relief that he hasn't offered to walk her back. What the hell is he up to? Certainly not a friendly lunch.

It's still brightly sunny at five past six, when Trish leaves the office. She turns right at the door, toward Oxford Street, and runs smack into him. Joe puts his arms around her and kisses her on the mouth. She feels his unforgettable body up against her new belly. She kisses back.

"I won't do this."

"I can't lose you, not ever again. I've made terrible mistakes. I love you. I am the love of your life and you are the love of mine and we should be together. We should be together always. You know it's true."

"I'm having a *baby*."

"Oh God, I know this is awful, but you belong with me. You, your baby, all of us together."

"That's ridiculous."

"No. It's tragic, and people will be hurt. I know you. I'm sure Nick is a special person. But you aren't his the way you're mine. He deserves more and so do you."

"I'm having a baby, Joe."

"Who will be the most loved baby, the most loved person the world has ever known. It's crushing to have it happen like this, and it's totally my fault. But it will work out. It will."

"I have to go. I have to go right now. This whole day never happened. You're a bastard."

"Do you love him like you loved me? Patricia."

She starts to run. She can't help herself, and it doesn't matter. What counts is to get away, out of his force field, away from all his tainted air, so she can think straight, and remember, and know what's real and what is nonsense, danger, poison.

She can't stand the thought of the tube, she wants to be home at once, to look at and touch all their things. She watches for a taxi as she walks and sees one coming free twenty yards ahead. She runs for it and has her hand on the door before it opens. A family of Americans gets out. She knows she won't tell Nick.

---

THREE WEEKS PASS, in what feels to Trish like a continuous out-of-body experience. Nick is solicitous, troubled by her mood and confused despite her best attempts to behave normally. She decides she's better off conceding things aren't right with her, and puts it on hormones, fear of the speeding future, the move, the speeding recent past. In her hopeful moments she thinks how really it's all true. Maybe these things are just attaching themselves to Joe and not caused by him. But when she tries to work it out in her mind she comes back to the irreducible thought that she hasn't stopped being in love with Joe at any time in the past eleven years. She's worked to accept a portrait of him—his manipulation, his ego, his cruelty—that is much truer than the version she defended for so long, despite the evidence. But the sickness, for all her effort, is still upon her. She doesn't know what she will do about it and prays for time to reveal the way. She loves Nick, and even more than her dread of hurting him is shock at the prospect of her own fall, committed knowingly, preventably, in slow motion. But she doesn't know how to stop it or, terribly, if she wants to.

They do whatever they've been doing of late. They work. They shop for the new flat and for baby things. They discuss finances and see friends and eat ice cream in bed in front of the telly. It's OK, easy, convincingly normal. Being with Nick isn't as different as being apart. That's when Trish starts churning. At least when they fuck, it's impossible to tell exactly what the difference is.

This just doesn't feel like her real life any more. This face, these arms, this cock? To whom do they belong? There's no continuity between Nick her dearest, Nick of the oysters, Nick of the Eau Sauvage (tacky in theory, but it suits him), and the man who's fucking her. If anything, and this scares her, it makes him sexier. Remembering their connection—the way it was when she could tell it was Nick up in her and she was Nick's girl—just blows the fuse and shuts her down.

ON A THURSDAY AFTERNOON Nick calls to say they're meeting Tommy for dinner, and where would they like to go? Somewhere different, and spicy, please. Nick has just the thing: a new Indonesian place opened up in Highbury, the Jakarta Club. They meet at eight-thirty. Nick has Tommy in tow from the pub. The Jakarta Club is crowded and jolly, trying too hard. They order beers and rijstaffel—lots of hot, sweet, peanuty things, festive and good. But it's oversold, so that for all the semi-authenticity they could be at a seventies fondue party, beamed forward with better tailoring. Nick and Tommy have done their talking at the pub, so Tommy solicits the banal particulars of pre-partum life with his straight, beautiful face. Trish is happy for the distraction, but at every pause the light goes out and she looks like a child on a railway platform whose mother hasn't turned up. The dinner ends sooner than expected, and Trish and Nick find themselves in the taxi home. They are quiet. Nick has an arm around her and she is grateful for it, but her mind is cratering. Nick thinks, this evening hasn't worked either. Later, Nick recalls the gentleness of Tommy's hand on his shoulder when they parted: an oncologist who doesn't need to review the file.

Back at the flat, Nick is half undressed when Trish calls his name from the sitting room. He comes in and sees her crying in the club chair, legs underneath her, arms on the arms of the chair.

"Nick."

He sits opposite her on the sofa, full of tenderness and adrenaline.

"I need to tell you what's been happening with me. I didn't mean to, but I don't know what else to do, and it just doesn't feel like I have any choice any more."

He watches her. She can't bear what she's about to tell him.

"I think . . . I don't think I'm in love with you. I mean, I love you. I love you to distraction. You are the single best thing that's ever happened in my life. But I don't think I was ever in love with you so much as desperately wanting to be in love with you . . . because I do care for you, so much, because you're so incredible, because we could have such an incredible life together."

She manages to keep looking at him as she speaks. A cubist painting of Nick is forming behind the still features of his lost face.

"Joe Somerville—I've told you about him—came and visited me at work a few weeks ago. I don't know how he found me. I was in Bond Street. He took me out to lunch. I wanted to be grown up. Fuck, I should be able to handle lunch, right? He's a hateful person. He told me that we should be together, that he can only love me and that I can only love him. I told him to sod off. I'd rather be dead if what he says is true. But the thing is, I think it is true. I should have known myself better. I should never have gotten involved with you, not so far, so fast. But it had been, you know, almost five years. A lot has happened to me in five years. I know what I know, that you are the best person, the loveliest, sexiest man. I was deliriously happy. You *know* that. But when I saw him it threw everything into a spin. I've been trying to work it out and I can't, I can't think properly."

"Trish—"

"I know. I'm having our baby, your wonderful darling baby. It's the only baby I could ever want. And we will carry on, and be happy in the end, both of us, for ourselves and for our baby. But . . ."

Here is a pause that neither of them wants to fill. He comes over to her by the chair, and puts his hand on the side of her face. She bends her head to cradle it beneath her cheek. Nick kneels down onto the chair next to her and they hold each other, and cry.

THEY DON'T GO TO WORK. They bump around the flat, barely able to walk, crying some, touching each other, talking a little. Early in the afternoon Trish goes out for a walk and calls Joe at his office from a pay phone. Yes, he means it. No, it mustn't be done lightly. Please, take the time, make the right decision. He will organize a flat for her at Dolphin Court, across the river from where he is. He loves her. She can think, and work it out in her own time. He is there for her, and her child, forever until the end of time, as he has been from the beginning of it. He will meet her at the flat at three-thirty.

Upstairs Trish packs her rolling case, as if she were still flying. She tells Nick she needs to go, to think. Yes, to see Joe, because how else can she figure this out? How else can she understand this madness except by confronting it? She'll call him in a few hours.

He lets her go. Is that the fatal mistake? What choice does he have? Don't go, Trish? Stay here and work it out with me? Weak. Refuse to let her leave? This is too real for gestures.

It's a day on drugs for Nick. Whatever is happening, however much he can't stop his mind from jabbering, it all filters through a body that feels diabolically altered. The nausea, the inability to get a breath, the edge of panic that won't recede: these are somehow the least of it. He just can't see around the elephant, because it looks like a different animal from every angle. Losing Trish, being left by Trish for her old flame, being blind-sided by Trish. Each is its own rich horror. But the future is more unspeakable still.

The child: Growing up where? With whom? Never knowing a true family? Or knowing it with Trish and the bastard? What if he's mean? What if he's wonderful? Will I be Daddy to my child, or the sad man it sees two weekends a month? And suddenly—Am I the father? Evil as it feels, is that the crusher or a ray of hope? No, he understands, the only thing he understands: that's not a hope. His mind has wrapped itself around this kid and will not unwrap.

Nick goes for a run to tire himself, to settle himself, to try to breathe. Light clouds today, high glare, and the neighborhood looks alien, as if the film has been treated. Is it worse than a death? Then, everything stops. Maybe the pain is worse, though he can't imagine how it could be. But at least there is an end, and then begin the consequences of that ending. Here it all goes on and plays out, and forever more—weekends, holidays, Parents Days at school—the characters, plus one, the star of this bourgeois tragedy, keep bouncing off each other, reshredding the wounds. Nick takes a bath. At first the scalding water is helpful, but as it cools, the tub—its Trishness—becomes unbearable, and he hurries out.

Trish calls, late afternoon. She's there. It's OK. She loves him. She's just so, so sorry. She doesn't know anything any more. Here's the number. She can't think, past the sad awful pain. Talk soon.

Nick's shattered, and now there are too many fault lines to follow and he feels panic lest he miss one, the right one. Like, how fast a worker is this Joe? Did he book the flat, knowing her so well? Or have they made more plans than Trish's pity for him will allow her to confess? Or is she just a fucking cunt? But what about what she said? Is there hope? Should he be fighting somehow? He's let the bastard move her a hundred yards away from him and now he's over there tucking her in, and probably tucking in. The hope is if she doesn't know her own mind. Now he must fight, be on her doorstep, be in her face, surround her with roses, be strong as she falters, we'll look back on this horrible day and— No, he needs to be strategic, right now when he least feels that he can. He needs to give her space. Stay put, stay steady, leave a light burning so she can find her way back, no blame, no questions ever, all's forgiven, the important thing is that you're home. You're home. He needs to wait, show patience, give her room, give her respect, but also have a presence. Some element that is him must be there with her, to remagnetize her, to bring her north again. What more can he send than what he's put in her womb already? She must work it out. But he has to give her something—symbolic, solid, smaller and sillier but less ambiguous than the child growing in her belly, who might not even—but what? Not corny or cute, not flowers, but nothing over the top either. They haven't even been together long enough to have their own secrets, their own traditions. A plate of oysters from Scott's? Great. Think of me and throw up. And of course she's going through hell too. He knows that much, he can hear it in her voice. If only he could think of something to do, some move to be present but not intruding, but more than a memory. A note. A piece of jewelry and a note. A crucifix, she's a Catholic girl, after all—lapsed, but surely torn, today. A beautiful crucifix and a note that says we are connected for all time. He'll buy it and send it over first thing tomorrow.

He calls Johnny, who answers on the first ring. "I need your help. I need your taste. Can you meet me tomorrow morning?"

"Yes. What's—"

"I need to buy a beautiful antique crucifix."

"Meet me at the top of Sydney Street. There are a few places we can try."

"Ten o'clock?"

"Fine. Nick? Are you OK?"

"No."

"Do you want to meet now?"

"I can't. Tomorrow. Thanks."

"I love you."

"Thanks."

NOW HE REALLY CAN'T CATCH HIS BREATH. It isn't a heart attack. Is it a panic attack? He's heard of those. Why not? Why not either? He tries to stand upright, holding on to the bookshelf. Breathe calmly, in through the nose, out through the mouth. He sees his hand on the bookshelf. It looks like a photograph, in this light. What? Go to the pub. See the lads. Tell them about it all, over a pint. See what he makes of their faces. He dresses himself, too warmly for the weather. He needs to right now. He hasn't eaten today, and he needs to do that too. Toast? How will he bear toast, without Trish? Will anything belong to the world again, and not to her?

The boys aren't there when he shows up. He gets a Bloody Mary and a bag of peanuts and sits in the small garden, consuming them. Tate turns up first, bringing a second Bloody Mary and his pint. He tells Nick about how he sold two Jags this week, one to a reporter and one to a nice Iranian who's something in advertising. Tate doesn't rush the stories. He likes to get the arc. Nick knows that Gorman's already heard them because otherwise Tate would be waiting for a quorum, which is what Nick is doing. Gorman appears and takes orders. Nick switches to bitter, with a double measure of whisky on the side.

"Cheers! Have you been at work today?"

"No. You're a good detective."

"You don't normally go home to change, do you?"

"No. It hasn't been my best day." This earns Nick the floor. "Trish has gone. Says she still loves her ex."

"Fucking hell. You must be miserable."

"I can't think straight."

"Nobody could."

"She says he came to see her a couple of weeks ago, out of the blue, after five years, to say she belongs with him. He's seen the error in his ways."

"Bastard."

"All those hormones. She doesn't know, Nick. You've got to remember that."

"Yeah, she's been up and down like a yo-yo for weeks."

"So where is she?"

"Gone off to have a think about it. He's got her someplace near him."

Both of their faces register how bad it is.

"That's a problem."

Tate shakes his head. "Kill the shit. Hire someone. No question he deserves it."

"No question, but where does that leave her? Loving me or mourning him?"

"Time takes care of many things."

Nick gets up to buy his round but Tate pushes him down softly. "No you don't. Same again?" Tate goes off, head shaking.

"You must feel like hell. What kind of man would do a thing like this?"

Nick adds the hanging thought. "And what the fuck is she thinking of? It's all Barbie and Ken now, but there's a kid on the way."

Gorman shrugs; it's beyond his experience, or almost anyone's. "She's off her head, but she's pregnant. Who knows what goes on with them? Now, him? He's got no excuses. He woke up one morning, had a coffee, read the paper, and said, 'Today I think I'll shit on the lives of three people.' As easy as reaching for the marmalade! I know I'm right, because how else do you do such a thing? Suppose the shoe were on the other foot. You find out that the love of your life is married, and about to pop a kid. It's been five years. What do you do? Maybe you go get pissed. Maybe you step in front of a lorry on the M1. I don't know what you do, but I know that you don't do this."

Tate comes back with glasses and three more bags of nuts. Nick feels a little better. The boys are with him, speaking logically, as if his car had been stolen. Nothing they say makes any sense but he admires the effort. Gorman tells a joke. Tate tells a dirty one and Nick even laughs. Nick doesn't want it to end, but it's coming time. They offer Nick their guest beds for the night. Gorman suggests a curry down the road, and Nick accepts. Gorman and Tate go to opposite ends of the garden, still in perfect earshot, to unmake their plans for the evening, conveying the enormity of events to those who await them. The world understands the priority of such a crisis. Why doesn't Trish understand it?

Down the road to bhaji, vindaloos, mattar paneer. They eat and drink too much, working it over between them. Time to go home. Nick thanks the lads and heads down his road. In the flat he turns on the telly before he turns on the light. He gets a bottle of lemonade from the fridge and parks it on his lap, watching an old movie with Alan Ladd in a fedora. He wonders which side of the river she's spending the night on.

TRISH ALWAYS FIGURED that her mother would have fucked Joe if she could, so if she winds up with him she knows her mum will applaud it. Mrs. Taylor is charming around Nick—charming is what she mainly aspires to be—but she doesn't get him. He's too kind, too straight. That makes Trish love him more. Mum, a practicing Darwinian, would have to prefer Joe: richer, handsomer, quicker. As she thinks these thoughts, Trish piles the pillows behind her and sits up to look around the odd little room.

What is she doing here, and how does she feel about it? She checks the clock—nine-twenty. She's slept late. It's Saturday, so Joe won't be going to work. And where is Nick? Explaining it all to Koestler over smoked fish and eggs? Running it off on a football pitch? Punching the walls in their flat? It must be a weird place now—weirder than here, thanks to what she's done.

Trish has a history with odd little rooms. The years at school and the years flying, dorm rooms and hotel rooms. Usually shared with someone else, another girl or two to cadge a fag or a tampon. Later there might have been a man, if she'd found someone suitable for a fuck. And ashtrays, tissues, a dead Campari-and-soda brought from the bar, another parched slaggy kip, interrupted by the alien peeping of an unfamiliar alarm clock.

She wishes this were one of those mornings in one of those

rooms, a parenthesis in an anonymous journey, with yesterday's pantyhose chucked on the chair and today's dress the only thing hanging in the closet. No fear of a phone call, save from the wake-up operator.

Trish wouldn't stir. The world out there would do the stirring for her, and in time present its idea of the future. She wants to cry. Not for Nick, not for herself. For a dream that won't ever be what it was—nothing will ever be sweet that way again. And for the little amphibian swimming laps in her unlit pool.

Last night was . . . what? Joe in his tender mode, making tea and even grilling plump fresh sardines on the dollhouse stove. She made the move. Fucking Joe again was the essential first step to working out the rest of her life. He's still good, beyond question the best she's come across. The prodigy has even matured, but she's willing to wager that he only showed her a little, leaving himself somewhere to build. You don't throw years of fresh material into the preview.

She can't help being cynical, though she knows Joe really means it. He wants her back, truly, wants to marry her, take on the kid, have them be his life. But he hasn't got the range for the notes. Smart, funny, strong—even sentimental—these Joe can be. But there's something missing in the soul department. That's Nick's category, and he runs away with it.

Trish wonders: Have I answered my question yet? Despite some things she knows—how Nick is the person who could love her and whom she could trust in a way that would never be possible with Joe—she doesn't feel any closer to the answer.

She doesn't regret fucking Joe. She could never regret fucking Joe, and Nick's heart is broken already. The other thing she knows is: the person she wants to walk in the room right now is Joe and not Nick.

And there's the knock on the door. Trish goes to answer it, dragging a sheet.

"Hi! How did you sleep?" Joe carries flowers, and a bag of groceries, and the leash of a gorgeous black dog at his side. "This is Marley. She's two. Marley, meet Trish."

Marley explodes into the room, tail beating, greeting Trish and sniffing around and coming back to greet Trish some more.

"You darling!" Give the man credit. He doesn't quail at the obvious when it helps his cause.

"Marley's a sweetheart. She loves children."

"How long have you had her?" Trish won't be surprised at any answer under three weeks.

"Since she was a puppy. Maggie's bitch littered and I took Marley for Clive's sake." Maggie is Joe's sister. Clive is Maggie's ten-year-old.

"How are Maggie and her lot?"

"They're very well. She asks about you." Trish and Maggie always got on.

"OK, so what's in the bag?"

"In the bag, we have . . ." He presents the items one by one. "Croissants. French butter, the Échiré stuff. Blood-orange preserves, made by Staud's in Vienna. Ground coffee. Milk. Champagne—Dom, 1985."

"And?" Trish watches his hand dawdle in the bag.

"A very large tin of beluga. And a spoon to eat it with."

"What a good boy you are!"

Joe comes up and puts an arm around her. She knows that whatever she thinks about it, this part will always be electric. Joe studies her face, and with a finger traces along her jaw, her cheeks, down her nose. He puts the finger in her mouth and draws her mouth to his. He backs her into the bedroom, keeping his lips against hers. He gets into her pajama top, holding a breast. It's as warm as a dove. He turns onto the bed, pulling Trish down on top of him. He can feel that she is twitchy with wanting him. Joe lays her hand on his penis.

"Put it in your mouth."

It's all she was thinking of. The prick still tastes like the first prick she tasted—which it wasn't, by two. Trish sucks it and serves it, hanging on to him while she does herself with two fingers.

Trish takes her wet middle finger and digs it up Joe's bottom. She curls it against his prostate like he taught her, back when she was just a girl. Coochie-coo. Joe comes down her throat. She rolls off, stretching out her neck and jaw muscles.

"That took you long enough."

"Fuck." Joe rises to kiss her.

Trish notices Marley, placid, in the corner of the room.

"Trained, I see."

Joe is up, organizing breakfast. Trish lies in bed, not moving much until the smell of coffee calls her. They wolf most of the eight ounces of caviar off the mother-of-pearl spoon, drink the Dom, and keep going on the croissants.

"What shall we do today? I mean, should I stick around? I don't want to crowd you."

"Thanks. I don't know."

"The thing is, I've got to be away tonight, at a client dinner in Paris. I'll be back in the morning."

Joe draws his hand fantastically through her uncombed hair.

"Oh, OK, I—"

"I love you, Trish. I want to spend my life with you. I hope you decide you want that too."

"Why don't we take Marley for a walk?"

"Sure. It's nice out."

"Just give me a minute."

"Right. But—Trish?—don't bathe, OK? I want to smell us on you. It's been a long time."

NICK CAN'T FIGURE OUT what to do with his day. Too much drink, smoke and food made for a long and bumpy night. By eight he realizes he is awake, with a weight on his sternum that will not allow sleep to return. He is relieved in a way, because waking up to remember the state of now would be much worse than this twilit, hung over business of never escaping it. Maybe she'll come home today. Maybe she isn't coming home. There is really no instrumentation to measure any of what's happening, and guessing is pointless. Is there something to do about it? Some action he can take? Hasn't he been over this already?

He thinks back to last night, and before that, and remembers he's meeting Johnny in South Kensington at ten. Nick gets into a hot bath and scrubs himself with the sudsy thoroughness of a child. He arrives at the top of the Fulham Road with half an hour to spare and goes into the Brasserie for a plunger of coffee and some scrambled eggs on toast. It all tastes amazingly good. He looks at the *Times*, scanning for coverage of something he can't quite remember—isn't there some big story out in the world, something he's following that mirrors his own disaster, only he just can't get his brain around it?

At ten of, he walks over to Sydney Street. What if this was just a normal Saturday, when Trish was flying and he was kicking around town? That couldn't be, of course, because Trish isn't flying any more, because Trish is pregnant. Will the baby be a boy or a girl? For a minute he tries to picture them living apart, and it being a little boy, and then the same but it's a little girl. He can't bear to think of it. He smacks himself on the forehead, as if to knock the ideas from his head, but really because his face is feeling hot and he doesn't want to start bawling.

It's not because he's meeting Johnny. In fact, he thinks, there is no one better for him to go to pieces with. Johnny would be patient and dear and have good instincts—better than his own—about little things to help. And after all the years of meltdowns and breakdowns and fuck-ups, Johnny owes him, and Nick knows it's a debt she would be honored to begin repaying. Probably that's a thought for later. Right now he'd like to avoid feeling the heat on his face, avoid the panic, acknowledge it, just keep the marker. Except for a plate-sized area over his chest where he can't breathe properly, and a baseline nausea, and something else he can't put a name to, he is feeling OK. If Nick falls apart prematurely, that's a form of surrender—and what he wants to do is fight.

He always forgets how tall she is. Catching sight of her where Sydney Street runs into the Fulham Road, he is surprised again by it, and by her goldenness. The movie star grin lights up when she sees him, approaching from the direction of Pelham Crescent. She's wearing jeans, white tennies and a white tee shirt, with a sweater draped over her neck. I could be taken for a lucky guy, he thinks, shaking his head. What if Johnny had wanted me? What if she was carrying my child, and we were together, and today we were going out to pick birth announcements? What if Marcus' father had never left Damascus and Nick did his thinking over tea in the bazaar? But then he wouldn't know Trish. How's that for an unbearable idea? Johnny comes up to him.

"What's the matter, Nick? You don't look well."

Nick explains. He is brief, and tries not to look at Johnny's face as he speaks. So—to the errand. "Does that sound like a good idea?"

"Oh, I think so. I'm sure you were right not to phone her, not to crowd her now. But you're also right that you mustn't just leave it her move. And the crucifix I think is a good choice. You must drop it off today, with a short note that says just what you feel."

"I'm not sure I can do that in a short note."

"Then subordinate content to form."

"How about 'I love you. Come home'?"

"The important thing—oh dear, I'm about to show my inner workings—the important thing is to stay out today. Really, you mustn't be there when she calls. She will call, because she sounds like a decent sort and I'm sure your gift will move her. But it's not as if the thing will do its work right away, you know? She isn't going to open the box and say, 'Krike! A cross!' and ring for the minicab. It needs to be given some time. Just don't let her spend her compassion. Turn off your mobile."

They find the right thing in the second shop they try—small, with sapphires sort of the color of Trish's eyes, and not too expensive, nothing that will overwhelm or seem intended to woo her. Nick gets a piece of paper and an envelope and writes, "God's speed. I love you."

They take a taxi over to Dolphin Court, a poky, mistressy place. Nick leaves his parcel with the porter. They take the taxi on to Campden Hill Square.

"What have you got in the house?"

"What's your wish?"

"Martinis?"

"Gin or vodka?"

"I think gin today."

"We've got gin, we've got vermouth. Olives or onions?"

"Olives."

They go down to the pillow room with ice and glasses, entering into a rite they've practiced since their teens. There is music—Miles Davis, *Get Up with It*, and Bobby Womack, *Communication*—from among many records he's bought for her. They lie back on the pillows. Johnny puts Nick's head on her lap. They drink half a bottle of Bombay, sprawled out upon each other. It's too arousing to be chaste but too chaste to constitute sex play: a suspended state, one without the weight of consequences, floating on booze and Miles and Bobby. Johnny is wonderful, she smells wonderful. Her skin is a wonder. Nick tries to count the wheat-colored hairs on the back of her neck between her ear and her tee shirt. Johnny pulls Nick's shirt up and runs her fingers around on his back, giving him chills for what must be an hour. Nick is in a state of erotic attention but manages to never quite get hard.

These are the games of their adolescence. His whole life, Nick thinks, he wanted this girl as he has wanted no other. Now that's no longer true. In this drunken vale of skin and gin, he draws an ice cube over his lips and licks off the dew. Today, maybe not for the first time but for one of the first times, Johnny is the one who would like it to move forward. Nick won't let it. Not because of Trish: nothing could make his heart any more or less broken. If anything, fucking Johnny would restore balance, which might induce the gods to reunite them. Johnny wants to now, because at last she doesn't love her. So the bigger things she can't give—to anyone, she fears—do not form an inequity between them. She could hold him without hurting him, maybe make him hurt a little less. But even if there might now be a parity of desire, and maybe even a parity of sadness, the natures of the desire and sadness would still not be the same.

HE GETS HOME VERY LATE. When he checks his answering machine there are no messages, just a bunch of hang ups. Soon after he arrives, the phone rings.

"It's me."

"How are you?"

"I don't know. Nick, it's beautiful. It's so beautiful."

"I'm glad you like it."

"Look. Can I come over?"

"Of course."

"I won't stay. But I want to—I can come in the morning if that's better."

"No, come now."

It takes her less than twenty-five minutes. Nick is sitting in the big chair when she walks into the flat. He sees Trish in the hall, lit from behind. No one ever looked like this. Nick tries to control his happiness.

"I miss you."

"I missed you too." Trish leads him to the bedroom. She turns out the light, takes her clothes off, and puts Nick on the bed. His prick is pointing up toward his head. Trish takes it in her hand, kisses it wet, climbs on, and gets it into her. She fucks him, leaning back and working against him, falling forward, her black hair around his face. She kisses his mouth, she kisses his eyes. She kisses his mouth. The lights of passing cars refract across the walls and ceiling. Nick feels the bumpy details of her insides around him. She comes on top of him and keeps riding. He tries to hold it as long as he can. As his come and his love and his sadness and his hope pump out of him into her, she grinds down and comes again, crying.

"I love you, Nick. I'll always, always love you."

She gets up, more quickly than he expects, and gets herself dressed. She is sobbing, beside herself, and now he is crying too, watching from the bed. He starts to move but she puts her hand on him, five splayed fingers pressed against his chest. She shakes her head, nose running, sobbing still. And she opens the door and leaves.

Nick is shaky from the sex, and crying, and unable to think. He goes into the sitting room. On the table by the door is the box with the little crucifix. Next to it is the note. He opens it. Trish has drawn a red heart around the words "I love you." Below it she has written, "I don't know how to do this."

WEEKS PASS. Trish moves in with Joe and stops working. Nick goes to the Exchange, plays football, stops at the pub. He sees Tommy, he sees Koestler. Everyone knows what the story is. He packs up the flat for the move to Kentish Town. The idea of that still happening is another surreal piece in his life, more papier-mâché scenery. One day Trish arranges to come by West Hampstead with Joe while Nick is at work. They pack up her stuff and move her out. It's easier for Nick because at least his own stuff is in boxes too, but still he spends that night at Tommy's. Tommy is the perfect friend for a time like this: kind, distracting, superficial until asked. All he says is, "Any time you want to talk about it, right?" And though he bats his baby blues, he means it, and Nick is grateful.

But he can't talk. He's talked to exhaustion, and would talk still, except for the clotted remains of old words that stuff his mouth. The monologue continues anyway, endlessly, waking and sleeping. How could he have been so stupid, to believe in a fairy tale? What kind of loser falls in love and gets married in a month? Trish was too beautiful to doubt, too beautiful to be a loser herself, to be so sad, sick, and dangerous to know.

Doesn't everyone believe that God occasionally gives such gifts, if only to prove he's there? How else could miracles happen? Who wants to question it, to say, Probably this isn't a miracle, just a pathetic consensus of wounded souls who are desperate to believe? Life is a flip-book of disappointments. Who wants to say we aren't going to be fine after all?

SO NICK VISITS JOHNNY'S PILLOW ROOM every few days for vodka, tequila, rum, and more gin. Sometimes they drink until they're sick, stumbling and laughing like teenagers, and then Nick holds Johnny's golden hair as she pukes into the toilet.

THERE ARE REALITIES TO BE FACED, but only a few so far, and no talk of solicitors yet. Nick cruises on a funereal high. He just feels ill the whole time. Nick speaks to Trish on the phone but doesn't see her until they meet for coffee before the OB appointment. The place, off Oxford Street, masquerades as a Paris café. The waiters are French, but it has only them and steamed milk in common with the real thing.

Trish is waiting when Nick arrives a little after four. She looks different. She's plump, and the belly has become a delightful thing, big and hard. Mostly there's just something more cooked about her. The skin is blotchy; the eyes are softer. Or is it that she looks sad?

At first Nick strikes Trish as the same as ever. But she observes the reappearing frown, the unease in the muscles around his jaw. He has this new thing when he listens, where he sucks his upper lip under his lower lip, like he's trying to keep the wheels from coming off. She hates what she is putting them through.

"How are you feeling?"

"Quite well. It gets harder to move around with this basketball in my pants. And eating can be an adventure."

"It suits you though."

Their waiter arrives as a gift of mercy, and they order coffees.

"What happened, Trish? Really, I need to know. Whatever it is, whatever actually went on, you've got to tell me."

"It's what I said. I wish there were more, just so I could understand it myself. When it became clear that you were—please try to understand this—it's as if you were a fantasy. You, the idea of our life together. And Joe is my reality. He always has been, I'd have to say. But I didn't know it until what happened. Every morning when we were . . . I'd wake up, and it was like that Dionne Warwick song, 'I Say a Little Prayer'? But . . ."

"Do you think you were ever in love with me? I know you said . . ."

"Oh Nick. Oh Nick. This isn't what I want to tell you, because it doesn't help, I know. But of course I was. I am. Can't you see?"

"I don't get it, I don't get any of it. If—"

"I made the terrible decision. And as terrible as it is, it's just the right one. Even though I love you, I'm sure of it. I'm sorry, but I know it's true."

"You aren't helping me."

"I want to. You are the dearest person in the world. I think about what you told me, you know, about the morning after your sister died? You talked about how you woke up, not remembering for a second. And then you know that the world has changed forever, and you have changed, from the knowledge of it, so now neither the world nor you can ever be the same again. I know that's how this must be for you, because it's like that for me. Those weeks before I left, I was trying to work it out, to fight it, to choose the best truth. But it wasn't possible any more. What's best is different from what's true. I'm sorry for myself, I'm sorry for you, and most of all I'm sorry for this one here. But I want to tell you. I loved my dream, the dream I got to share with you. And I'm not sorry that I didn't wake up before. Despite everything, I'm happy—can I say happy? I'm happy for this." She puts her hands on her belly again. "Because of what it means. And now I want to know this one, our one. I want this child to exist."

Nick can only whisper, "Is it mine?"

"It's absolutely yours. I have no reason to say it. I don't need any help from you, or for you to be the baby's father, but you are. This is our baby, yours and mine. I am certain of it."

"OK." Nick breathes. "I think—I know we weren't going to, but with everything, we should find out if it's a boy or a girl."

"I was thinking about that too, and yes I agree. Also, can we not go into what's happened with us? I don't want to deal with all of that with them. I don't want to explain it. I don't want their faces to be sad. It's not their business. And, Nick—you'll be with me when the time comes, right?"

Nick nods his head. He can't stop himself from crying now.

"It's our love that made it. We'll bring it into the world the same way."

They walk over to the OB's, awkwardly, because they want

to hold hands but they don't. Nick feels nervous going into the place, like he's acting a role and people can tell; but no one notices. The technician rubs jelly onto Trish and puts the ultrasound wand against her. She describes what they are seeing on the monitor, a healthy and obvious human.

"We've decided we'd like to know the sex."

"All right, then. Let's have a look. There's the pelvis. There's the right leg. Can you see it? And there's the left. And in between, in between, no— It's a little girl!"

"It is? Are you sure?" They are smiling and crying, just like they all do, and Nick grips her hand.


HE MOVES INTO KENTISH TOWN on a Saturday. Johnny comes over to help, and by two o'clock all the stuff is in. They wait for the deliveries—the crib, the pram, a tower of brightly colored boxes. The baby's room is white and butter yellow, with blue and white curtains, all the things that Trish picked out. Nick and Johnny push the furniture around, and then Johnny opens some boxes in the kitchen and finds what she needs to make tea. Nick sets up the sound system.

"Do you mind if I spend the night in Campden Hill Square? I'm not ready to do this."

"Oh, my dear. Stay as long as you like."


THEY SIT ON THE SOFA UPSTAIRS, watching Clint Eastwood videos, drinking Brouilly and eating enough McDonald's take-out for six people. Part of the way through *For a Few Dollars More*, Lucy rings Johnny. She's in the neighborhood. She and Koestler have just finished dinner. Yes, Nick would like that.

They make their way through the ashtrays and McDonald's wrappers and climb onto the big sofa.

"How did it go?" Koestler asks Nick.

"It went fine. I'm sure that one day I'll even have the strength to live there."

"It won't be a sad place," says Lucy. "Babies make everything happy, even when that doesn't seem possible."

Tonight Nick believes it could be true.

A GOOD AUTUMN GIVES WAY to rainy cold. Solicitors' letters are exchanged. It's a surprisingly easy business, when nobody's got any axes to grind. Early in December, Nick is called off the floor in the middle of the morning session. Important message from Mrs. Clifford. He hands over his positions and steps outside to call Trish.

"Nick? Wait. Can't speak." After about a minute the contraction subsides and Trish says, "Jesus, Nick. You wouldn't believe it."

"Are you OK?"

"Yes. They started early this morning and now they're coming about every seven minutes. Can you meet me at St. Hilda's?"

"Yes. How will you get yourself there?"

"Not a problem. I'll see you upstairs."

"Here we go!"

"Yes, here we go."

Nick finds Trish in a small waiting room on the maternity floor. She is alone, huge, owl-eyed, with a pathetic little tote bag next to her on the floor.

"How did you get here?"

"It was fine." She wants to tell him not to worry, that Joe is taking good care of her, only without putting his name in the air. For everyone's comfort, she's had him leave so that he and Nick needn't meet in the middle of all this.

"What's the plot?"

"I'm meant to wait a few minutes for a room to be prepared. They're six minutes apart, which is how long it feels like they last. I should be about a minute and a half from the next one."

"How is it?"

"There's no mistaking it for anything else."

"How can I help?"

She looks at him, thinking about it.

"Trish, we're here. I'm here to help. You do the work and I'll do what you tell me to do. Whatever it is, it's OK. OK?"

"No, I know. OK. If you don't mind—" She tightens with the upward slope of the pain, tries to relax into it. "Just kind of support me by my arms. I'll show—" She can't speak any more. Her back is to Nick. He holds her weight with his hands under her elbows as she tries to go as limp as she can everywhere else. It isn't good. She twists away wildly and reaches around to clamber up him. Nick loses his balance with the shifting weight and it nearly sends them to the floor. She puts her arms up around his neck and just hangs off him, like a drowning sailor.

It's fine for Nick—all he has to do is stand there. And to feel her there against him, her arms, her beautiful, capable hands, the smell of her. The contraction passes and Trish unwraps herself, unsteadily.

"That was better."

Whatever the mess they find themselves in, this is clear and right and on the topic. A woman is giving birth to a man's baby and the man is there to take care of her. At least this part is as it should be. They do one more contraction in the waiting room. A nurse arrives to tell them that the birthing room is ready.

It takes about half an hour to move in. Trish has to get undressed and settled on the bed, and wait for the monitors to be put in place, and get some questions answered. As each contraction begins, Trish rolls off the bed to hang from Nick's neck, her feet planted wide on the linoleum beneath her, timelessly. The OB, a round, cheery Persian woman, checks in to examine her.

"Good. Three centimeters. Excellent work."

"Ta."

"How's the pain?"

"Painful."

"They do a lovely epidural here. I recommend it."

"Waiter!"

The OB smiles. "I'll send in the anesthesiologist for you."

Nick speaks up. "What do you think? About how it's going?"

"It's going well. This will take the pain away, but not the full sensation. You can watch the contractions here." She points to a monitor. "Tell her, because she may not feel them, and she'll want to know she's progressing."

The OB trades a we-must-give-them-something-to-do shrug with Trish.

"How long—"

"I assume nothing, because it can work out quicker or slower than you expect. But she's off to a good start. What can I say that will not mislead you? Between an hour and a day, probably. You could start a pool."

The anesthesiologist arrives with the cart of goodies.

"Please step outside—just for about ten minutes."

"Wait!" Trish yelps.

Nick takes her hand as if she were Ginger Rogers, and Trish rolls into position to ride another one, gasping and hollering.

"See you in ten," Nick tells her.

"Thank you. Thank you."

Three more hours, three more centimeters, general discomfort but not shrieking pain. Nurses come and go, administrators, everyone jovial and chatty. This, thinks Nick, is the bit of a hospital to work in. And, he wonders, mustn't everyone have that same thought when they're in this room?

Trish asks Nick about his friends, and Kentish Town, not secretively but not within earshot of the staff either. Nick feels almost normal reporting it all. He doesn't ask Trish about her world.

Four hours, still six centimeters. The OB smiles.

"I think we'll break your water. That may move it along."

"Isn't it moving?" Nick asks, for both of them.

"Yes, yes, it's fine. But this may help a little." It's a two-person operation, and a wet one. The thing looks like a chopstick. "Nice. Look at all that amniotic fluid. A very healthy, well-protected uterus. Remind me—did you find out what you're having?"

"Yes." Trish perks up. "It's a girl."

"Any names?"

"Not yet."

They had never revisited the old conversation together, but as soon as the others leave they dive into it.

"Do you still like Charlotte?" Nick asks. It was the name of Trish's favorite aunt.

"I do, but is it too done? There seem to be a lot of them around."

"There will only be one of her. Charlotte Clifford sounds like a heroine from an adventure novel."

"Doesn't it? Like a Katharine Hepburn character."

"Or a Joan Crawford one, if we're not careful."

"It actually sounds quite posh."

"It will 'til they meet her."

They smile at the thought. Trish nods.

"Charlotte what? Charlotte Grace?"

Nick smiles, his eyes tear up. "Do you think?"

"Yeah."

"Do we want a third name?"

"Now that, surely, is a bit posh."

"But maybe we should put Taylor in there."

"I don't think so." Trish is definite.

"So—Charlotte Grace Clifford?"

"Yes."

Trish looks at him and they share the quiet.

"Nick? I hope she gets your eyes."

Six hours, eight centimeters. It has become night without them noticing, and a quiet rain is working outside. They watch the news on television. As troubled a day as any to bring a child into the world, and no worse than most.

"Are you OK?"

Trish is not OK. The labor is wearing her down and the sad thoughts are making a home in the room with them. There are tears on her face.

"I'm so sorry about how this is. I'm glad, you know, but . . ."

"You're working. It gets to you. Your body is working so hard. And Charlotte is making her way. She's almost here to meet us."

"And what we've made for her."

He grips her hand. "She was made—"

"Yes, in love. I know."

"I know. Are you feeling ready for the next part?"

"No! But I'm well ready to be done with this. I want to meet her. I want to see she's OK."

Eight hours, and the room is changing before them, like the set in a modernist play. Trish is ten centimeters dilated and the baby has moved into the desired station. The pediatricians are on call. The OB has her kit arrayed. The lights are dimmed. She goes over the next part with them.

"So, my dear, are you ready to push?"

"Uh-huh."

"Start on the next contraction. Papa, watch the monitor and talk her through it. You're clear?"

"*Alles klar*," says Nick, in a nervous burst of war film German.

Nick has got one of her legs and the new nurse has the other. Without thinking about it he kisses the top of her foot. Trish smiles at him.

It begins. Calling, coaching, screaming. Trish sweats and farts and squeezes Nick's arm, but she sails through the work, confident, one with her purpose. An hour passes quickly, the four of them sharing the intensity of it. Now during the contractions Nick can see an oily black mass in Trish's pussy.

"That's your little girl's head. Of course she's wet right now. What a good hard worker!"

Her head mostly disappears after the contraction. It appears again with the next one.

"OK, Mum, push! Give it everything, push!"

The contraction subsides.

"All right, this next one. Get ready. Beautiful work, let's have a beautiful finish. Nurse? Call Peds. Let's deliver this baby."

The next one comes. Thirty seconds of blind effort and Trish pushes the head out. Immediately, more reptile than mammal, the long little body slithers after it. A second, a second, a second, OB clearing the mouth, a second, and they hear the rich, irate cry from beyond the foot of the bed.

"She's a beauty." The doctor holds her up—mucky, squinting, gorgeous. Trish's and Nick's hands never stop squeezing each other, amazed, and they're crying too, and grinning the fundamental grin. They aren't paying much attention as the cord is cut, or when the afterbirth follows, on the next contraction.

The little person is cleaned, bundled, and moved to a table in an adjacent alcove. There the pediatricians work briskly, and one calls out "Nine." Gazing and clasped hands and sweaty kisses and the OB sewing away down below.

Again, "Nine."

"Great scores," says the OB. "Twenty inches, six pounds eleven ounces. Textbook, my dear. Textbook in every respect. Congratulations."

"Can you bring her to me?"

"Sure, Mum. Try to nurse her."

She puts the child on Trish's chest. Trish smiles at her baby and holds her. She smiles at Nick. Nick kisses his daughter's face.

"Hello Charlotte, Charlotte Grace. I'm Mummy. And this handsome fellow is your Pa."

# PART TWO

he two days in hospital are an oasis of uncomplicated joy. Then Joe brings Trish and Charlotte home. Now they must work out some kind of a way to be. Nick suggests that he meet with Joe for a drink, to face up to the weirdness. Joe knows that his move is to be responsive, and accepts. He thinks of it as a stand-up thing for Nick to do. They pick a pub in Kensington. Nick wants to be able to walk over to Campden Hill Square after the ordeal, and puts Johnny on notice. Nick leaves the Exchange immediately following the session, to beat the rush. When he arrives at the Mandeville, Joe rises from a table to greet him.

"Nick. Joe."

On the way over Nick was remembering things Trish had told him about her first love, back when it was her history, and not his future. He's thought about it a lot these past months, and now here is the person to square it with. His first unpleasant realization is how good looking Joe is, certainly better than Trish wanted to say. Beautiful suit, handmade shirt, no tie, hair a little wild. Not the kind of handsome that other men laugh at, and not pretty, like Tommy, but a compressed, intelligent energy. Of course he's devastating to women. Strong jaw, strong handshake, not out to prove anything. The eyes are a little small but alive and sharp.

"It's good to meet you. What will you drink?"

"A pint of bitter, thanks."

Joe is drinking Guinness. "Congratulations. She's amazing."

"Thanks."

They move to a table, computing each other.

"There's a lot to say and nowhere to begin, is there?"

Nick watches him.

"But I'm very glad you suggested for us to meet."

Nick accepts that he wants to deck the bastard. And he can't think of an alternative, or recall why it is he shouldn't.

"Maybe I can say a few things. The first is that I'm sorry about how this happened. I was stupid and wrong to wait such a long time, but I was hurt too, by what happened between her and me. And it's unforgivable that as a consequence so much harm was done. Having said that, I know Trish has zero regrets about being the mother of your child. You should know that I know that she loves you and is proud of the fact that you are Charlotte's father. And you should know that I respect that too. I will always love them both, and protect them both, in every way, to my last breath and beyond. But she's your daughter, and I won't ever forget that. Whatever our feelings, the awkwardness and, I know, a lot more, you will always be welcome wherever Charlotte is. I mean that. You and I may not like this, but here we are. You're in my life. I'm in yours. And as to Charlotte, I'll always remember my place, with her and with you."

"I will hold you to that."

"Fair enough. Now about Patricia and me. Think what you want to about it. I don't blame you, but I can't help. I did what I did because she belongs with me. I didn't vandalize four lives for sport. Trish and I were practically born together and—I assure you—we will die the same way. I truly believe that we were destined for life, or I would never have asked her to make the choice."

Nick stands up and gives a little bow of the head. "Thanks for the drink." He turns to leave.

"Because, Nick—she chose."


AT JOHNNY'S HE FINDS a bottle of Stoli in the freezer. He pours a small glass of the plasma for her, and one for himself. He puts the bottle back in Siberia and sits on the kitchen floor.

"Was it OK?"

"Fuck!" It's a frail holler. "What am I going to do?"

Johnny crawls over to him and keeps going, head down, until she bumps into his chest. She rubs her head against the front of his shirt. He gets his fingers in her hair. She turns her face to his.

"Come upstairs. For a cry, for a lash."

"Why? Because I need it?"

"No. Because you're beautiful."


TRISH MEETS NICK in Kensington Gardens, on the wide promenade running south to north. Charlotte is in her pram, well swaddled even though the day is warmish for December. They have gotten together twice this first week home, both times on neutral ground. Nick loves to see his girl, and whether she's awake or asleep the visits mostly consist of looking at her, holding her, talking to her. When Charlotte is awake, she's usually alert, if not precisely focused. She is comfortable in his arms, home with the smell of him. When he nuzzles into her and whispers the first verse of "People Get Ready," he can feel her body relax against him.

"We need to talk about arrangements."

"Of what kind, Trish?"

"Of the you and your daughter kind. She's too little to be away from me, you can see that."

"Yes. Of course."

"You're welcome where we live. I know Joe told you, but I want to tell you too. And we're planning to move. Hopefully closer, to Islington maybe. But I think that in the meantime we should visit you in Kentish Town. So that you can change her, bathe her, really spend time."

"That would be great. Thank you."

"Whatever you want—evenings or weekends, I'm assuming. Of course when she's a little older she'll be able to stay with you. This way she starts getting comfy in her other home."

"Right."

"As to the arrangements, the solicitor matters, they seem to be on track, don't they?"

"Yes, fine. Look. There's really nothing for me to say to you. I met Joe."

"I know."

"I don't like him. And I don't like you. You ruined everything. And please don't fucking explain it to me one more time. You've hurt me, unbelievably. And this—I can't get my mind around it. I don't understand. Life was unreal before, fairy tale unreal, and then it became nightmare unreal. And now—I can't even describe the kind of unreal it is now."

"I'm so sorry."

"This is my baby, but I don't put her to sleep at night. I don't believe that anything will ever make sense again, not for me. What you did, how you did it . . ."

He shakes his head and it turns into a shudder. "Really,

Trish. I don't believe any of it. How we're sitting here—you, me, the bench, the bloody trees. None of it, except Charlotte."

She is a red face under a pink hat, asleep on a fast darkening day.


CHRISTMAS, NEW YEAR, CHRISTENING. In the families of newborn Charlotte Clifford, they are tests of strength and measures of conduct. Elegantly planned for minimum friction, and stoically observed, they put Charlotte's adults on their best behavior. The Cliffords, Taylors and Somervilles pass smoothly between church and the festive rooms where champagne is poured. There arise many opportunities for theater, or at least discomfort— Johnny and Trish, Nick's and Trish's mums. There are even entertaining undercard bouts like the Koestler and Trish rematch, or Tommy and Johnny, who share an abbreviated secret history. But nothing gruesome occurs and the holidays pass in a hush of good manners, mostly with record-setting brevity.

The hardest one for Nick is Christmas. It's the first, and the one about which he, like every new parent, has fantasized the most. For his future family he had pictured intimate settings of touching affection—nothing but the manger and a circle of golden light, as Koestler teased him: ideal mother, attentive father, radiant child.

The practical question now is where to have it. Kentish Town would be too painful. Joe's flat is inappropriate. Doing it in the country, at the Taylors' or Cliffords', is awkward, quite a trek for a day when no one wants to linger.

They wind up at the Taylors', best of the bad choices, only forty minutes out of town and not a place that promotes intimacy even among its residents. The plan calls for morning mass and a buffet lunch. Its execution is cleanly ceremonial: everyone's in a car by three. The toasts naturally are short—God bless Charlotte Clifford, good health and long life. Things that everyone can say and mean and not feel worse.

New Year's is an easy nothing. Joe and Trish bring Charlotte round and raise a glass in Kentish Town. As soon as it's over, Nick bolts for Johnny's.

The christening is back, by general agreement, at the Taylors'. Charlotte gets baptized according to the Roman rite, the Taylors being Papists of the casual modern style. The day is not as strained as Christmas, since the principals have already done it once. But with more of a supporting cast, there is greater potential for color. Nothing happens, of course, and the thing goes on until nearly six, pleasantly, with all sorts of odd pairings— Nick's brother William and Johnny, Tommy and Joe—talking small and amicably and sometimes at length. The anticipated confrontations never occur or occur blandly, everyone being grown up and no one caring to bring a lit match into the gasworks.

But Trish and Johnny get to appraise each other. Johnny makes it a point to dote on Nick for Joe's benefit. Joe, predictably, is so impressed by her that it puts him in a foul mood. And what further riles him is Tommy, and the way Trish flutters when he comes over to chat. But the darts are rubber-tipped. Everyone says that the day went well.

It's tough the first time Trish and Charlotte come to Kentish Town. Here they are together in the house they intended for the three of them. But the baby needs nursing, the baby needs changing. A baby structures the day. Nick has loaded the place with amusements, though Charlotte is too little for them. A bouncy seat hangs in the kitchen doorway. The garden is full of premature plastic vehicles. By their third visit, Trish starts to feel comfortable—the place was her idea, and so is most of the stuff in it.

"So is it OK for you, coming here?"

"It's nice."

"Her things make it nice."

"I was thinking, actually, that Charlotte looks more moved in than you do."

"I know what you mean. But I'm getting there."

She asks after Nick's friends and family. "I've meant to write your folks a letter. Not so they'll think well of me, God knows."

"They think well of you. They're philosophical."

"I did send a thank you for the lovely presents. We need to see more of them."

Trish wonders if Nick is with someone. Johnny, probably. She can tell that part of his life is elsewhere, and it feels funny, even though the more he gets on with it, the better it will be for all of them. She knows she has no right to feel anything. Her life is good. Even when she's here with the two of them, she can't picture it having turned out any other way than it did. She can't imagine not being with Joe. His family, sister, friends—some of whom were her friends, before—have embraced her. They'll have a nice house, and a country place, maybe a farm in France. Does Nick think she was trading up? Is that how he sees it? She hopes he knows her better than that and thinks he does.

Leaving Nick for Joe will be the defining decision of her life. But define her how? She left her husband and ran off with their unborn child. But when you allow for history, it's more like Nick was the affair and Joe the marriage. She only thinks this way after she comes here.

Now that she is back with Joe, their old issues haven't really changed much. But Joe's changed, no doubt about that. She got his attention. And he's brilliant with Charlotte. Sweet, funny. He really loves her, and Charlotte loves him back. But Trish is also sure that Charlotte knows who Daddy is. She recognizes the voice, the smell, the blood.

Trish takes the sleeping baby from Nick's shoulder and puts her in her crib upstairs. When she comes back he is still sitting on the floor, back against the sofa, looking out into the garden. She sits down next to him and lays her head on his shoulder.

"May I?"

"May you? Trish."

"What?"

"Fuck off."

JOE BUYS THEM A BIG HOUSE in Islington. They move in the spring. Nick buys a car, an Audi, so that he can get around with his little one. It's weird, the first time that he comes to visit Charlotte in the new place. But at least Joe's not around, and the fact that it's still only half finished makes it less of a trial. Nick says that this will be a nice home for his daughter to grow up in.

And there's the dog. Marley is sweet around Charlotte. Nick has a weakness for Labs. It's too bad that Marley's master is his nemesis. He wishes he could see a time when Charlotte has a dog at Daddy's.

ANOTHER WEEKEND, and Charlotte is asleep in her crib in Kentish Town. Nick and Trish are downstairs, without a lot to say to each other. Nick asks if she wants a cup of tea. It's a warm day for April.

"I'd love a Coke, if you've got one."

Nick returns to the sitting room with two Cokes. Trish is on the floor with her legs stretched out in a vee. Jeans, black flats. She pushes off the shoes and clenches and relaxes her bare toes. She smiles at Nick.

"You always fancied my feet."

"They're good. You know it."

"Them and what else?"

"You've got a lot of good features. But you do happen to have excellent feet."

"Yes." She looks down to study them. "They're a source of pride and comfort, I must say."

"Trish? What are you doing?"

"I think about it. I'm sorry, I have no right but I do."

"Well, don't."

"Anyway, you can tell, can't you?"

"Don't."

Trish pulls Nick over by the front of his shirt and kisses him. Their mouths are sweet and cold from the Coke. What's going on? Is it wrong to do this if he wants to? Certainly he wants to.

"Yes, yes." She says it from under his wild kisses. "But it means what it means, yeah? It doesn't . . ." She undoes his flies, finds it and pulls it out. "Hello."

Nick stays put, head shaking—shaking away thoughts that would prevent this from happening, shaking away sanity and self-preservation. Or is his body right to accept the bounty?

Trish lies down alongside of him and rests on one elbow to get her head over. She holds his balls with her free hand, swallows his dick and sucks the come from it. They remain stretched out on the carpet, not speaking. It's quiet time, minus the juice and cookies.

NICK IS STILL ANGRY, but now that's only a part of what he's feeling. What's the point of what just happened, for Trish to reassert her dominion? Unnecessary, her power is clear. And he really doesn't believe that's the point of it. If Trish thinks she went back to Joe in a tectonic righting of her world, then this too is a putting right, another cataclysmic sin to realign the plates. Even though he knows this act changes nothing about where Trish and Charlotte will live or whom they will live with. The two of them lie together while their baby sleeps her sugared sleep upstairs. Nick is sad, but calm, in a way he hasn't been since all of this started. Trish must know that.

What is Nick's life, beyond the afternoons when the lights are on in Kentish Town? The job, the friends, Johnny, and all the unmarked hours spent alone. What does it mean that these water bubbles are everything, and that now, with this, he's OK about it?

They spend each Saturday together in Kentish Town. While Charlotte naps, Trish and Nick float through the temporary universe of the sitting room. Often the French doors are open to the garden, admitting springtime, and the sound of birds and neighbors' tellies. When a tooth is working in and Charlotte is fussy and won't nap, Nick and Trish can't make angels on the carpet. So they take her for walks, or give her a bath to distract her. Usually Trish goes out to do some shopping in the neighborhood, trying to stay away so that Nick and Charlotte have the time alone.

Nick loves these hours with his girl. Charlotte is never anxious, delighted by the goofy man-toy that is Daddy. Sometimes he takes her into the garden. A leaf, a flower, a handful of grass or some dirt is all he needs to transfix the observant little face. Just keep it moving, Da. Sometimes he puts her in the pram and pushes her around the block, feeling impossibly completed. Twice on their expeditions they run into Trish. A big happy greeting, a head turned in question, but no tears at "bye-bye."

Nick gets plastic covers for the electrical outlets and a safety latch for the cabinet of poisons under the kitchen sink. He buys child-care books, *What to Expect the First Year* and Penelope Leach. He talks with Trish about what foods Charlotte can eat, fine and gross motor skills. He has complete trust in Trish's un-stressed competence with the child, and it doesn't surprise him, though he can't figure out where it came from. But it's more than maternal nature. Managing is Trish's great gift.

When they put Charlotte down for her nap they look at each other to ask the question. Then the carpet and the sofa—never Nick's bed, where another language might be spoken—draw them down on each other. He wonders what it means, and how it reckons with Trish's love for Joe. He is sure on only two points. He knows not to talk to her about what's happening between them, and he knows that Joe has no idea. He would be insane if he found out, no less than Nick would be if the joke were on him. Does this mean he wins? No, because the girls still leave, and for six and a half days he drifts alone across his shallow planet.

And though the sex is unlike anything he has ever known, true oxygen, it comes with conditions. It's ravenous but not or-nate, because they never have the time. And they never speak, and rarely look at each other, because then they would be facing the treachery. And maybe then she'd stop.

NICK GOES TO DINNER at Campden Hill Square. Johnny is cooking because her brother Con is in town. Con dresses in expensive girls' clothes, like the Milan update of a seventies rock star. He is still trying to kill himself and still kept by rich friends. Is he gay? Constantine Colson is pretty enough to be a girl. He's got his sister's skin, only waxier. He's got Johnny's famous blond hair and old scarves. His chopped up jeans are a thousand pound art project. Con always has his assignments—aborted opera design, aborted magazine launch, aborted love affairs with German princes and princesses, aborted suicide attempts years old but still accessorized with gauze wrist bandages. Shrieking poofter scenes involving blood and alcohol, but never poofters, except possibly Con. Does Nick have a problem with that?

Back ten years, a cloudy Saturday afternoon, and young Nick and young Johnny are snogging—desultorily on Johnny's part—in a big armchair in the sitting room. Out of nowhere Johnny howls, "Con! Go away!" Nick turns to look. Con has crept into the room and seated himself in the opposite armchair. He is leering, with his erect penis in his hand. "Put it away and get out!"

Nick perceived that this was no unusual event *chez* Colson. And he wondered, or realized that he had always wondered—does Johnny fuck Con, or does Con just dream about it? Con is in love with his sister, and Johnny's sadness is connected to that love. Con laughs at Nick's straightness, at his loyalty to his Johnny dream. But the Nick and Con show isn't funny now because there is no truth left to illuminate. Now the stage is bare of anything but longing.

Still, it doesn't take two to tango. Con keeps trying and Johnny is too protective to make him stop. Her own spent brother-love has turned to pity. And it's by way of pity that Con has fallen and Nick risen to comparable values on her emotional stock market. As always, she just wishes they were friends.

Johnny's dinner is some kind of delicious poached coquillage, then spring lamb, white and enrobed in cherub fat; minted peas and parsley potatoes; Sancerre followed by Forts de Latour. Everyone has reasons to drink too much.

"So I gather you've finally moved in, Nicholas. Congratulations." There is no response, so Con perseveres. "My lovely sister has come to her senses after years of fraternal pleading. She won't do better than you, and at last she sees it. But it's different now for you, isn't it?"

"No, Con. I'm still just trying to get to you."

"Oh God, if only you meant it. But you've always been secretly cruel. No one would believe me until now." Con spears Nick's rack of lamb and holds it before him like Yorick's skull. "I'm just a poor little lamb who has lost its way."

"Fortunately, I'm good with children."

"Why of course! Of course you are! Do you have any pictures of the angel?"

"No, not on me."

"You're a rotten thing."

"I just don't need you fashioning any dolls of her, not before she can walk."

"Sister, should you not have browned this fat? How are we meant to eat it?"

"You're not meant to eat it. It's *agneau de Pauillac*, you're meant to cut it all off."

"Cut it all off? I've been working up to that my whole life. Is tonight the night?"

"Enough, Constantine. Please put down my rack."

"You've always known, haven't you, Nick? Johnny's healthy as an ox. It's just the ankles that fool you. I'm the sick one, the only sick one. Johnny got all of Mum's sensible genes and I got all of Daddy's bad ones. That, and he fucked me when I was little. What? He did! Turns out he never laid a hand on her, wasn't his line of country, as it were."

"Seeing you again it all comes back, the same old crap. Like getting my car clamped."

"I love my themes. Is that so bad?"

"It's so tired it hurts."

"It hurts all over. All over and all the time. But you hurt too, don't you?"

"*Basta.* I'm done with this. It's been a long day in a long weekend, in the middle of a long year. I concede, *con*cede. I'm not up to it. I can't play with you tonight. Sorry."

Con's face changes and his eyes fill with tears. "No, I'm sorry. I know I can't imagine. I only wanted to amuse you, but as usual I struck the wrong tone." Con gets up and leaves the room.

Johnny looks at Nick and smiles. "How was it today?"

"It was fine. It's been fine lately. Sometimes I'm still knocked down by the realization that this is my life, but it is. I'm learning little things. For example, I've found it's harder when they leave me, and better when I drive them back. I think if Charlotte were sad it would be unbearable, but she's still so small. She's happy to see me and happy to go. It's all about Mummy now. And when that changes, I suppose I'll be more ready to face it."

"Daddies are the whole story for little girls. I think I can speak on this. And if it isn't perfect, you won't be the exception.

What matters is who you are. She'll cry and miss you and wonder about all of it. But you've got a true heart, as true as anyone I know. Charlotte is blessed, and that can't be changed, ever."

"I hope so."

"You love her, and you won't ever betray her, not on purpose."

"No, never."

"Well that's the important thing. You're with her again tomorrow?"

"I'm taking her to visit the parents. Just me and her."

"And how will that be?"

"The folks and I are getting along OK. And I love to be with my little one."

Johnny's eyes moisten as she smiles at him. "You're good with girls. That's the whole point of you."

They look at their wine glasses.

"I want to be good for her, more than anything. I've spent my life in howling devotion to the skirts—yours, mostly—and now I need to look after one of my own. But I don't know how I can do it right when I understand so little. I mean, less and less all the time. The last year has left me speechless."

Con sticks his head through the door.

"Did I tell you? I'm doing a Buñuel night upstairs. *Viridiana*, which I've loaded, and *Obscure Object of Desire*. Are you coming up?"

"In a minute."


SUNDAY LUNCH IS A FIRST—putting Charlotte in the car seat and driving out to see Grace and Marcus. William is even down from Warwick. And it will be Charlotte's first whole day with Daddy and no Mummy. Nick has made a tape for the car ride, and also brings a CD of songs that Trish has given him.

They head out on the M3, Charlotte content with a plastic clackety toy. It feels funny to Nick that the child seat faces backwards. He can't really see her, just the top of her head. But he talks to her, telling her about her grandparents and uncle. The first song on his car tape is Johnny Nash, "I Can See Clearly Now." Nick sings along, trying not to drown it out, thinking it's good lively music for a little girl. Two minutes in and he sees her head is over to one side. Asleep—good, child. He waits to the end of the song and turns the music off. Father and daughter, out for a drive.

The Cliffords live in a cottage on the green of a thatched village mostly taken over by weekending broker types. Like the others, theirs is very old and very small. But Grace and Marcus are neither original locals nor occasionals. They have made their home here, so the place has a quality, both put together and worn in, that's different from the others on the green.

William is in the guest room. Grace is in the kitchen doing a full Sunday roast. Nick pulls up and Grace comes out to greet them, calling through the house as she goes. Nick lifts Charlotte out of the car, still asleep in her detachable seat. She starts to stir, curling and stretching.

"Hi sweetie. Wakey wakey. We're here."

"Oh, she's precious! Hello little one, hello Charlotte Grace."

Nick smiles, and brings her out of the seat and into his arms. "It's Gran. What can we say?"

Charlotte looks around warily for the one who is not in view, but she isn't ready to cry.

"You've had a good kip, Sha Sha. Now we're in the country."

William and Marcus watch from the front door. Marcus,

even after three years, even at his leisure on a Sunday, still does not have the right shoes for village life. Nick thinks, I mustn't get trapped into going to the pub with him. Once, they gave him the benefit of the doubt there, despite his plush pullovers and wrist bracelet, his Bally loafers and Agio cigars. Now they've heard through his lies but they still have to look at him, still must say hello to their own Smyrna merchant. Yes, anything but the pub.

"Dad, hi! William, how are you, you great brute." William is not a great brute, and knows it, but is happy that Nick says so. The brothers hug, encircling a bemused Charlotte. Grace has gone in to check the meat and William makes for the bag of baby things. "You'll find the wine back there too."

"And very nice," says William, fishing two bottles of claret from behind the back seat.

"So, Pa, how is it?"

"Very good, very good. Interesting developments. How are you?"

"I'm well."

Marcus is running through his repertoire of funny faces for Charlotte, and she is just what he likes, an easy audience.

"Come inside. Let me fix you a drink."

There is a cycling race on the television. Marcus mixes Bloody Marys for the men.

"Cheers."

"Cheers, Dad." Nick wanders into the kitchen with Charlotte. "Ma, can I get a pan of water to warm a bottle?"

Nick balances Charlotte on his hip. He has found that if he stays busy she will ride on his arm like this for hours, taking a quiet interest in everything that passes her vision.

"Oh Nick, she's such an angel."

"Isn't she?"

"And she's beautiful. With two boys, we never had a beauty in the family. She looks like you, and Trish as well."

"She looks like Trish."

"But with your coloring. And your mouth."

Nick holds her up facing him and smiles, and she grins back a gummy grin.

"Yes you do!"

"Nick, I feel like I never get to tell you, but I think about you, about how you're managing. And I wish we could see more of this one!"

"I know, Ma. It'll get easier. She's just seven months old and it's hard working things out. I mean, this is the first time that Charlotte's really big enough for us to be off on our own like this. Soon we'll be able to come for the weekend."

"I can't tell you what it means to have you here."

Grace maintains her contact with Charlotte, smiling and flirting, not aggressively, reassuringly, drawing her out, so that as she passes close Charlotte reaches to go to her.

"See, Ma, she knows her Gran. Want to go to Gran? OK!"

Nick hands her across, staying nearby so that Charlotte knows she's safe. Charlotte has no problem snuggling into Grace's shoulder.

"You should see her face, Mother."

They stand together in the small kitchen, mother, son and granddaughter. The baby plays with Grace's hair as she holds the bottle for her. No one feels a need to move until Charlotte speaks up, pointing to the glassed-in cupboard full of painted crocks and teapots.

"Eh, eh."

"Well let's go look, shall we?" Grace walks over to the cupboard.

William comes in from the sitting room. "So it seems better, Ma."

"It is, I think."

"Pa's latest catastrophe?" Nick asks William.

"It doesn't look like they can proceed against him."

"Wouldn't that be a relief. Not that he deserves it. But you do, Mum."

"Yes I do, don't I? And I think I deserve a snuggle too. Snuggle snuggle snuggle!" She puts her face in Charlotte's belly, and Charlotte laughs.

"She's lovely, Bruder." William tries. "And such a lot of hair. What color are those eyes?"

"I'm told it's too soon to tell. I hope they stay blue, like Trish's. Trish says she wants her to get my green ones. With all that, I wouldn't bet against brown."

"They're enormous, whatever they turn out. And look at those lashes!"

Grace adds, "That's Trish. I always said, she's like a young Elizabeth Taylor—and this one too."

"As long as they don't end up like old Elizabeth Taylors." William exits on his quip.

"How is Trish, dear? How are you, with everything?"

"OK. Strange, but that's the only way it's ever been, really. And I can't say why, but I feel that things will stay all right between us. We make the best of it, and there doesn't seem to be so much of the tension. Not like when it first happened—I was ready to pop. But then you say, 'What's the point?' This is how it is, we make the best of it."

"It's wonderful that you can be so wise. It's more than I could ever be."

"I don't think so, Ma. You're who I learned it from."

"Well, I've put up with a lot. Just don't hold yourself to an impossible standard. It can back up on you."

"Uh-huh."

"OK. Take this sweet girl, give me ten minutes, and I'll have lunch on the table."

Nick calls, "Shall we go for a stroll, William?"

"Oh sure. Dad, you coming?"

Mutterings from the settee.

"Didn't think so. Come, the pram's in the boot."

They do the green. William goes on about his studies, lodgings, stalwart friends, ski holidays, grand plans. It's all the same, Nick thinks, the same for everybody. If they sent down an efficiency expert from a business school on Jupiter, he could write a stunning monograph. Such endless, unnecessary replication on this planet: the same narratives, emotions and results, all creating nothing except a desirable circulation of income.

But how would I feel if I were not still fucking my wife? Probably rotten, as rotten as I felt before she started fucking me again. Not for my ego's sake—after all, she still chose him. She's just like that, so I happen to benefit. If she hadn't dumped me for Joe, she'd be doing him on the quiet and lying to me. So I guess she's loved and honored, at least.

Lunch is one of Grace's classic efforts. The baby eats little bits of potato and mashed-up vegetable with gravy. Nick feeds her while she coos and devours and smiles around at everyone. Marcus drinks too much but not much too much. The afternoon passes better than Nick could have hoped and then, sleekly, they are back in the car. William gets a lift to the station. He's still boring, still endearing on the great subject of his life. Fear not, my brother. Your contents too will settle during shipment.

Charlotte sleeps most of the way but wakes up irate. Nick debates pulling over to give her another bottle. First he tries the tape of baby songs, with no joy, then his own tape. She may turn out to be a Van Morrison fan.

It's still light when they arrive back in Islington. Joe meets them at the door and invites Nick in for a drink. Trish and Marley hurtle down the stairs to greet the gurgling child.

"You had fun with Daddy! And Daddy had fun with you!"

Charlotte beams back at her mother, in love and complete. Everyone heads up to the sitting room. Marley nudges Charlotte hello, and checks Nick out. The place is looking nice. Joe behaves well, relating to Charlotte but respecting the genetic geometry. Nick wonders, is he more of a Daddy when I'm not around? Do I want him to be, or not? Trish asks after the Cliffords. Nick describes Charlotte's day. He's sure Joe has no idea, but how could that be? Doesn't Joe know how Trish is, better than anyone?

Maybe that's the point; maybe in some ways Joe knows her and in other ways he is blind to the things Trish prefers unseen. So how important is it that he is fucking her? No question that it's cleared some of the tension between them: I fuck my ex because it makes us better parents! How important is it? It's important, however sad that is. And now it hurts less, for him. Does it make it hurt less for her too?

From Charlotte and the Cliffords, the conversation moves on to property—prices, weekend property, nicest counties, ease of driving. Nick had no idea Trish knows so much about it, and can't imagine why she does. It must just be that this is the kind of conversation that occurs in this room.

When Joe and Trish ask Nick to stay, with good simulations

of warmth, Nick pleads a previous engagement, takes up his Charlotte, puts his face to her neck and breathes deeply. The bigger she gets—the more aware, the more participatory—the harder it is to leave her. He misses her little reactive looks, her sounds, and always the heft and warmth of her.

Everyone is fairly pleased to have behaved decently. Nick leaves the house with waves and bye-byes, passing through the emotional airlock to his weekday world.

In fact Nick does have a plan. He drives down to Knightsbridge, where he meets Tommy for a pig-out at Mr. Chow's. Because he's already had a bit to drink, he orders Coca-Colas with lime in big iced glasses. They gorge on lettuce-wrapped pork, fried seaweed, pot stickers and Nine Season prawns. It is a festival of brazen gluttony such as two unaccompanied men can conduct in town on a Sunday night. The assault is marked by good humor and slight topics, and bigger topics chopped down to size: Tommy's mother's and Nick's father's drinking, Nick's sense that Trish's life with Joe, while charming and comfortable, is not more exciting than was Trish's life with him. He thinks—but does not speak—of the complications in this phase of his ex-marriage, its odd architecture, the Rorschach design of the double-cuckold. He pictures Trish splayed naked, her pussy raised and raw at the center of the inkblot, like a Schiele painting emerging from the stain. He thinks that this X-shape, this double-cuckold, would make someone an excellent coat-of-arms.

TRISH IS OUT FOR LUNCH with Joe's sister Maggie, at a very nice restaurant in Neale Street. Maggie is off work for a few days and staying with them in town. Having her friendship again is a bonus to being back with Joe. Maggie is older than Joe by two years. Thin, pretty in a tough way—well, maybe not, maybe Trish just likes her. Maggie is confident, structured, real without being literal, funny sarcastic, but never cruel, like her brother can get. And Maggie has always liked Trish, and Trish has known it.

"So how do you find him?" she asks, over Kir Royales.

"I find your brother mostly the same. Perhaps he isn't as angular as he used to be."

"I think you're wrong about that. Breaking up your marriage and dragging you back with child in womb is pretty damn angular, wouldn't you say?"

"You don't approve."

"Certainly I understand. But it was quite cruel of him to make you choose. And I understand your choice. It wouldn't have been mine, but I don't blame you for it. You feel what you feel. I just wonder what made him show up in your life, then. You never would have done this off your own bat."

"So what do you think it was?"

"Bloody minded arrogance. Though I know he's as serious as he can be about it. He'll be a rock, for you and for Charlotte, no monkey business now. But what a thing. To realize he's made a mistake and set about fixing it with no concern for the mess. And I'm sure in his mind he believes, 'That wasn't so bad. Put your head down, charge through the shit. It's worth it to put things right.'"

"I suppose I'd rather look at it as a greater force that commanded him. I'm the one who chose, after all."

"That's funny, that you hold yourself accountable for your actions—as well you should, you made a hard choice, and God help you if it wasn't the right one. But you let him off."

"I hold myself accountable, but I have to tell you that once he faced me with the choice I knew he was right. There was no choice, just the truth—to deny or acknowledge. He makes me . . . I tried to see the good that would come of denying it. I did try, you know."

"I know. He told me. He was quite stressed."

Trish snorts a laugh. "Was he?"

"He was. But don't think he's lost any of his edges. They just wear a cardigan these days."

They eat their lunch and wander down around Covent Garden, spending their afternoon in the shops. Maggie gravitates to well-made things, attractive but not modish. Trish always feels immature out shopping with Maggie, and suppresses the desire to try silly adorable frocks she knows she'll never buy. Maggie picks up on it.

"Don't let me kill your fun. I shop like a man, I'm afraid. In that respect, Joe has always been the bitch of the litter."

"You don't shop like a man."

"I do. I pick from things I know I like. I shop as a chore, and buy with pleasure. Girls—like you, and my darling brother—take your pleasure in the shopping. You delight in testing everything that's possibly available, especially what you know you won't wind up with. And then the moment of purchase is more—it isn't necessarily a case of buyer's remorse, but it's a moment of loss. What matters is not gaining the acquisition but giving up all the choices you didn't take. That's why some people buy everything, two in each shade. So that every morning when they look in the wardrobe they get to decide all over again. If you aren't rich though, I'm sure it's easier being me."

Maggie is right about most things, and certainly about Joe. He loves to admire himself in his new clothes, he loves to pick out his kit in the morning, and he loves how his body moves inside his loose but precisely tailored suits. He's a bit of a fucking girl. She'd always teased him about it, right at the start. Does this explain the timing of when he decided to besiege her remade life? As Maggie also said about Joe shopping, he'll only choose when his options start to disappear.

SATURDAY, AND TRISH AND CHARLOTTE are in the garden. Nick has gone inside to organize ice creams when Trish hollers for him to come. Charlotte, who has been trying to crawl backwards but ended up pushing herself into a seated position, is rocking forward on hands and knees. Arm, leg, crash. Smile. Arm, leg, arm. Crash. Charlotte looks up.

"Da!"

"Hi, honey!" There are tears in his eyes. "Are you going to crawl to me?"

Smile. Arm, leg, crash. Arm, leg, arm, leg.

"Look at her! She's doing it!"

"She is," says Nick, edging forward to make the distance less. They meet in the middle of the small lawn and Nick lifts her into the sky, telling his girl how great she is.

"You know she saved it, don't you? To show her Da."

"I'm honored, Charlotte."

"It's so nice we got to be together for this."

A SULTRY AUGUST DAY in Kentish Town and no one has the energy for a plan. Charlotte cries herself down for a nap. There's usually a breeze from the garden, even if it's a heavy one, but not today. Nick is cranky and Trish isn't saying much. She sits in the armchair with a leg hanging off one side. As Nick walks by from the kitchen he brushes his hand against her hair. Trish turns her head, in what's meant to look like acceptance but is in fact a rebuff.

We can talk about our daughter. We can play with her and care for her. We can fuck. But I can't touch you. I can't show you simple affection. Am I not permitted to feel that too? If we were having an affair, I'd hold your hand in the restaurants where our friends don't go, but we're not having an affair. I don't know what it is we're doing and I can't ask, because if I ask then we're talking about it, and if we talk about it then it's real. I am pathetic, more pathetic for the gift I steal, the gift you smuggle to me.

Nick sits opposite Trish on the sofa. She should have just taken Charlotte home. What's the point of this, don't they have someplace useful to be? Trish gets up from the chair, walks out into the garden, and walks back. Nick's gaze follows, like he's watching the receptionist at an infirmary, dully but with an interest. Trish stops in front of the sofa and stands with her back to Nick. Her feet are dirty from the garden. She doesn't move as he pulls down her white capris and white knickers. Feeling lost, Nick stares at the sky-blue tee shirt where it meets the milky bum and slim legs. He kneels behind her and puts his hands on her cheeks.

He lays his forehead against the small of her back, as if in prayer. He eases her apart. She smells good, and specific. He puts his lips against her and kisses into her asshole the truths he may no longer kiss into her mouth. He thinks of the Commodores, Lionel Richie before he went kitsch, singing, "Just to be close to you, for a moment, for an hour." Just to be close to you. A heavy tear falls on his face, like the leaking relic in a Sicilian church. He works her butt to open it up to him. He eats her ass, and she allows her ass to be eaten, breathing delicately. He would swear she fills the room with the sweet pang of rising dough.

His dick is hard in his pants. He'd like to push her forward, spread that ass and roll it back onto his dick, do it like a porno, turn her out like the whore she is. But he won't. He may be hopeless, but not fucking her, not getting off, is the one small stand he can make.

It's however long it is, ten minutes maybe, until Trish understands that Nick is locked into her, lost, not going anywhere, just parting her like a worried dog. She takes a step forward, to break the seal. She picks her knickers up from the floor, puts on her capris, puts the knickers in her pants pocket. She turns to look at Nick. He's still on his knees, a midfielder watching the other side win by a penalty kick.

"It's hot," she says.

NICK HAS A DREAM. It's strange because he remembers it, assisted by the comfortless heat, and strange because it is so lucid, like a parable. There is a poisonous creature, either a small bird or some sort of insect, and the deal with it is that its venom is fatal, so you must cut off, or out, whatever it bites. The poison moves to the central nervous system and kills within a few minutes, and it moves perceptibly, spreading a slight numbness as it goes. The creature bites Nick on the fingertip. He runs to the kitchen for a big knife and tries to figure out how to chop his finger off, but in his terror he becomes almost comically flustered. Must get it while it's still at the finger, or I'll have to take the whole hand. I'll never be able to do that, chop through wrist and wristbone. He puts his finger on the cutting board and raises the knife over his head. I need to really hack it, one clean stroke. But the odds are that I'll miss and just carve myself up, and then will I be in too much pain and too freaked out for another go? But if I try to do it slowly—that's impossible, you can't cut off your own finger as if you were slicing a baguette. The numbness is up to the second knuckle—must chop—can't look—got to look—it's my finger! Must aim. Swing, but aim. Swing, but aim. He wakes up and stares around at the monochrome grayness. He wonders if he would have made it.

NICK HASN'T BEEN SEARCHING, but when he's approached about an investment banking job in New York, he takes it. The commitment is for a minimum of two years. He can afford to keep Kentish Town, and gets six weeks a year in the UK. He'll take the Friday BA flight out of JFK at 10:00 P.M. on alternate weekends, returning on the Sunday 4:00 P.M. flight. It will eat up whatever he's likely to net over his current take, and it means seeing Charlotte less often, but she's getting to the age when longer visits are becoming possible. It means seeing less of Trish. His feelings about this are more complicated than he wants to explore. When he discusses the plan with her she's eager to be supportive, mostly conveying her concern that the travel not be too hard on him. She knows he'll remain close with Charlotte. Of course, they will coordinate to be sure she is available during Nick's visits home.

It all reminds him of Trish leaving, because once things are set in motion they move more quickly than he had pictured. Even though it's his choice, the speed is a surprise, about ten days from agreeing to going. All Nick has to do is pack a suitcase. His London life will await him, unchanged. The realities—

of leaving the Exchange, for so long a friendly haven, of even fewer sessions at the old pub, of less time with Tommy, with Koestler, above all with Johnny—only sink in as he approaches Terminal Four.

What he can't prepare for is the thought of being three thousand miles from Charlotte most of the time. Pediatrician visits were generally reported to him, but when he could go it made a difference. He could stop by Islington after work with a toy and a cuddle, to cheer her up if she was fussy, or just to share her mood. That didn't happen much either, but at least it was possible. It didn't seem like such a gift until now.

What is his purpose in getting away? The life of the last year has been a non-life, revolving unevenly around Charlotte, Charlotte and Trish, incapable of sustaining any other substance. Professionally distracted; romantically possessed, while possessing nothing; bombarded with feeling to the point of anesthesia; Nick just isn't proud of himself any more.

New York is a place where maybe something else is achievable. Not a new life, he doesn't want that, just some of his spirit back. So now, instead of maintaining this painful shallow-space orbit around Charlotte's world, he will pass into and out of it, and make a place that can be his own, and unprovisional. How will two years in New York be less provisional than his life here? Who the fuck knows?

NICK LIKES TO TRAVEL. The inevitable inconveniences rarely bother him, while the timeless rhythms of International Business Class fill him with cheer: the eye-shades, the Burgundies you never heard of, the hot towels, hot cookies, hot and disturbingly moist assorted nuts. Why not warm—warm nuts, warm towels, warm cookies? Is it that they just can't get it right, or is excessive temperature the wink of artifice, like a hooker's moans? Intended or not, Nick likes the irony. How homey it can be, lying fully reclined next to fifty strangers in a metal tube hurtling over the Atlantic. But in truth, like every home he has known, it's as homey as the inmates conspire to make it. Maybe with Trish too, but for those few months they seemed to be working toward something more classically picturesque.

Nick eats the nuts, drinks the Bloody Mary, and adjusts his seat position, listening to a Dire Straits album he once admired that now never fails to put him to sleep.


NICK LANDS TO A BALMY SUNDAY EVENING in New York. Don, the driver of the town car, is full of information. Don drives Mitch Carson, the personal potential tycoon. Mitch doesn't know that Don moonlights when the big guy's back in Montecito. Tales are told of Mitch's byzantine private and professional lives, witnessed and deconstructed by Don. Nick gets to hear them because he looks like a nice guy. Or maybe because, like Don, Nick has a kid who doesn't live with him. Don is a free thinker and wants Nick to know that whatever Nick might prefer—in the way of entertainment, companionship, or pharmacological enhancement—would pose no logistical challenge. Don only hopes that Nick will have a good time.

They arrive at the Regency Hotel on Park Avenue. Nick is booked into a large and comfortable room. He calls Evan, from the office, who was hoping they could meet for dinner. He means it, even though it involves driving in from Saddle River, New Jersey, on a Sunday night. They meet at nine, at a steak house that looks like a giant garden shed on the outside. They drink Château Léoville, eat brilliant steaks, smoke Havana cigars.

Evan Goldstone is smart, self-mocking, and deeply competitive: the American version of an Etonian. They had met on several occasions before interviewing in London, but this is the first time he really gets him. Evan is excited because he thinks he and Nick will make lots of money together, beyond the packet Evan must already make.

Evan and Christie have two daughters, Cerise and Morleigh, nine and four. So the men do Dads and Daughters talk over the cigars and coffee. Nick notes the lightness of Evan's touch around the subject of the breakup, and tries to respond honestly but without appearing tender. He's ready for battle, and wants to come off that way.


IT DOESN'T TAKE HIM LONG to get sorted, settling into work and renting a light-filled apartment off Central Park West. He joins a gym full of gay men and preoccupied women. He uses the treadmills next to the stretching area, for their view of dancer types extending boa-like around big yellow balls. He doesn't try to chat anyone up, but he knows that amid all the gayness, and with the accent, his odds are excellent. He plans to avoid the tightly wrapped women on the elliptical trainers—trotting away under their yellow Walkman headphones, eyes fixed on copies of *Self.*

There's nothing at home yet except his bed, phone, stereo and television, so it's hard to think of this as real life, and he doesn't try. On nights when he isn't out with work mates or clients he orders up food from anywhere on the planet and watches a movie on pay-per-view.

Evan and Christie take Nick out with Christie's sister Erin. No sparks, as Erin says, but they like each other enough that Erin invites Nick to a gallery opening and lines up future prospects for him. Nick is flattered, repelled and baffled by this bear hug from near strangers, but he's happy for their help.

NICK SLEEPS ON THE FLIGHT EAST, and dreams he's being loaded up like a pack animal. It's a pewter-colored morning at Heathrow. At home he has a long hot bath. It's nice to find his place unchanged, nice to think he'll be leaving again for dreamland tomorrow. Trish arrives with Charlotte at two. He's struck by how different she looks, how much she's, not grown, really, but moved ahead, in two weeks. She stares at him for ten or fifteen seconds, until her face breaks into a wild grin. Nick wants to laugh and cry, but sticks to the former, sweeping her up, hugging and kissing his precious one and tossing her into the air. Trish sees his emotion and puts her hand on the back of his neck, moving down the tendons in the way he loves.

They go to the zoo in Regent's Park. Some of it, like the new tiger cubs in their glass-enclosed habitat, Charlotte can't really get. But she loves the gorillas, pointing at them and calling, "Dis! Dis!"

An ape looks back with the implacability of a Bucharest maître d'. Charlotte eats ice cream, which spoils her dinner of biryani rice at the Indian place. She chews on a naan and flirts with the older couple at the next table. Nick enjoys his tiredness, and being with the two of them. Not his girls, exactly—he hasn't the right—but one that's his and one—what? What is she? She isn't in love with him. He doesn't love her either, any more, not the way he did. So what is it, survivor bonds or inter-locking Stockholm syndromes? The kindly looks from the older couple disturb him, make him feel like he should explain the picture they think they're reading. But aren't they more right than wrong?

Nick expects to drive them back to Islington but Trish says, "Would you like her to spend the night? She pretty much sleeps through, you know."

"Could we? I'd love that."

"I'll come back with you to get her down, and you can ring for a taxi for me."

Nick phones to cancel a plan with Johnny. Trish organizes Charlotte's blankie and baby and sets up some bottles in the fridge, explaining the drill to Nick. He takes the lead putting her to bed—changing her, reading a bunny story, with Mum in the room blessing it all. The music-box mobile plays "Imagine." Charlotte drifts off.

"Look, if there's any problem, please call. I can be over in ten minutes and I'd rather I did than not. So that she'll feel comfortable here."

As they run this three-legged race unopposed to nowhere, it's tough to know where they're at. From the moment she walked in this afternoon, Nick has thought she wanted to sleep with him today, but maybe he's wrong, just wishing.

No. Standing at the door to leave, she takes his face in her hands and kisses him on the mouth.

"Do you want to?"

Why would she ask him that, to prove the proven?

"Yes."

Trish backs him into the room with hungry kisses. She's in

his mouth, tasting his mouth, telling him how good he tastes to her. She unbuttons his shirt. He's thinking, floor or sofa? But she takes his hand, like Wendy on an adventure, like old days, and leads him up the stairs, into his bedroom, onto his bed, once and once again theirs.

They take off their clothes. Nick lies on the bed and Trish gets on top. She doesn't stop kissing him, sucking his tongue into her mouth.

"Wait. Sit back," he says. "Let me look at you."

Trish straightens up, smiling. She's so narrow, so white. Smooth as sculpture, thighs astride him, strong thin arms, high breasts, that upper-case "I" in her belly button, the celestially registered trademark of the only thing he'll ever want.

She loves his eyes on her. She puts her fingertips on his nipples, traces around the chest hair, down to his navel, and gets a hold of his dick. She just wants him to look at her like that, the broad friendly face as gaunt as an El Greco martyr's.

Nick pulls her close to kiss her again.

"Darling. Here."

She gets underneath him and lifts her knees up.

"Fuck me like this."

Nick starts to go down.

"No, now. I'm so ready."

He feels how wet she is and puts himself in. He fucks her slowly, to record new memories for his future survival. She likes his hand under her head and the other one holding her ankle. The way he smells, the way he's doing it, he's all so much a part of her. She squeezes her toes to thank him for all that love. She can't make things right, she can't fix them, but this makes them better. It must, it's so fucking good. Right now, him in her, him on her, must be good. Fuck me fuck me, oh fuck it out of me, please.

"Nick, I'm going to—"

"I want to feel you—"

"Oh fuck. Get it, get it all."

The molten light spreads out of her, across the bed and down onto the floor, covering all of it.

"And you, I need to—"

"Uh, uh." Five, seven, ten jolts into her, how could he get any deeper, but he is, filling her, a rough yell with each punch, like he's the one getting hit.

"All of you, all of you."

"Trish."


SHE STAYS IN HIS ARMS for a few minutes. She kisses him. A minute more and she is up and dressing.

"Do you need anything?"

"Just a taxi. Nick?"

"Yes?"

"Remember—phone if you're even thinking you should. And if not, I'll see you in the morning around nine. She'll be up by six or six-thirty. You two have fun, yeah?"

He'd wanted to offer her a towel to wash up. Not to worry. As always, Trish has it under control.

What was tonight? Certainly, the whole day pointed sexward. Fucking in their old bed, the bed in which they conceived Charlotte. Does this make it more of an affair? What does he want from it: the idea, however fractured and conditional, that they are a family still? Is that OK to perpetuate? How full of shit could he possibly be? Trish only handles him so easily because he's so desperate to be handled.

Nick is too sleepy to keep thinking. And, he fears, too sleepy to hear Charlotte if she cries. So he takes the bedding into his daughter's room and gets comfortable on the floor next to her crib. He falls asleep with a tear in his eye. It's not bittersweet anything, just simple joy at the soft sound of mouth-breathing from his little girl above him.

IN NEW YORK, after a movie downtown, he goes to dinner with Erin and some of her friends at a restaurant in the Meatpacking District. The hostess is a tall skinny Indian girl with a blinding smile. The restaurant stays open until one on weeknights, so the next evening Nick comes back late, after a client dinner, with Evan in tow. They show up around a quarter to twelve and sit in front, where they can smoke, right by the reception podium.

The girl's name is Sareen. Nick asks her out for a drink after work. Evan heads home, pleased with his assist. When Sareen gets off she takes Nick to a bar down Gansevoort Street. She is from St. Louis, came east to study, transferred to NYU, went to Europe and came back. From the flow of the story she could be in her mid-twenties, but Nick figures her a few years older than that. She's dry funny, with the great smile, and fantastic hands, fingers of extraterrestrial length and delicacy. He wants to fuck her but Sareen explains, pre-emptively, that she can't ask him back for a drink because her roommate's boyfriend is over. Nick says he'll be away on the weekend, and says why. They make a plan to meet the following Monday, when she's off. Nick rides uptown in a taxi, happy for someone new to think about.

WHETHER IT'S BECAUSE OF HER AGE, or the sleepover, Charlotte is really connected to him now. At eleven months she's such a big girl. She chatters, greatly favoring the letter "d": "dis, dat, dada." She raises herself to stand and navigates the cocktail table with a drunkard's determination. The eyes, the wit, and the aspect are all her own, parts of her personhood, not just her childhood. She loves to joke and loves to flirt, but she is always clear about how she feels. Whatever her mood, you know it. She's got Trish's intrepidity and handiness, Nick's equanimity, with maybe a little of Marcus' cunning thrown in. Her skin is dark, like Nick's, but her straight black hair and deep blue eyes are Trish, if they don't change.

They have fun together on Saturday. Trish drops her off and picks her up, and Nick doesn't mind having the time alone with his girl.

He sees Johnny for dinner on Saturday night, and plays football with the boys on Sunday morning before his flight. He showers at the field house and entrusts his dirty kit to Tommy: true friendship.

He's looking forward to New York. The work, the energy of the place, new people he likes. He tries to summon that smile, and the praying-mantis fingers. He has more to look forward to. Koestler, on his way out to Singapore for the paper, will be in New York to visit the week after next.

On Monday Nick is excited, but fried. He feels uninteresting and awkward at dinner but Sareen doesn't mind, watching over the sleepy boy. They go back to his apartment. He is surprised by her modesty, and charmed by the sincerity with which it yields. Nick gets to see and taste most of what he's been thinking about.

So what's missing? Is it the perversity he's used to, the twisted emotions and quicksand sex? Is he just unaccustomed to the wholesomeness of it? Sareen is a wonderful girl, but he knows he won't fall in love with her. Maybe that's the good news. Probably it's just what he needs.

They spend more nights together. Nick hears about the restaurant and the yoga studio, and meets Sareen's nice enough circle of friends. She brings stuff to his place. She takes dance classes nearby on Broadway. And she cooks, not the searing Indian food that Nick is used to, but subtle, smoky northern dishes that her mother taught her. It's good to have someone in his kitchen.

KOESTLER ARRIVES NINE DAYS INTO THE AFFAIR. Nick has taken delivery of a pull-out sofa. Sareen stays at her own place so the boys can catch up. Nick and Koestler watch basketball on TV and talk about New York. At first they're serious, but listening to themselves they turn it into a cliché competition. People here are so unguarded. Everything goes twenty-four/seven. The coffee shops the newsstands the delis. Nothing you can't get delivered. Nothing an English accent won't get you. The Sinatra song is so true. They're shouting them at each other, gunning for trumps. When Koestler interrupts the essay "Sikh, African, and Haitian Taxi Drivers: Compare and Contrast" to exclaim how America's self-revelation is emotionally dishonest, the game collapses and Nick concedes.

After midnight they get a taxi down to Thirty-second Street. Koestler takes Nick to an all-night Korean barbecue. The place is crowded, efficient, and fairly dirty, with glaring fluorescent lights. A beaten-down old man brings a brazier of hot wood coals and sets it between them, into the sloshing foul hole in their table. A young waitress, marginally less servile than the brazier man, brings a big plastic tray from which she unloads a dozen small dishes—kim chi, dried fish, chili paste, several varieties of raw green vegetable, and sauces hot, salty, or sweet. Another woman, less bowed, brings an omelet of scallions and oysters the size of a Frisbee. She cuts it quickly, with scissors, and serves it to them. Finally a better-dressed woman, clearly senior, brings flat baskets of thin-sliced marinated meat. She drapes some across the smoking grill.

After their feast they walk uptown through the cold night, laughing and belching. Koestler begins, "Should I ask how you're doing?"

"I'm OK, surprisingly so. The job is good, Charlotte is— you've got to see her, she's brilliant. And this little thing I've lucked into here—"

"Bastard!"

"—is very promising."

"Well, I'm impressed. Delighted. Relieved. Relieved, delighted and impressed."

They pass out of Times Square and head up Broadway.

"But you have made it rather easy for yourself, haven't you?"

Nick doesn't answer. Fuck him.

"Fair enough, easy's the wrong word. But how excellent that you could just levitate out of the whole mess."

"What? Don't I get to live as well? I'm back every two weeks, jet-lagged and baffled, but I'm back. It's fine. It's best for everyone."

"I suppose you asked her. 'Goo' means 'Daddy's a jet-lagged

zombie'? 'Goo goo' means 'I don't mind, as long as Daddy's happy getting rich, and getting his end away'? 'But Mummy, why does he always smell of papadums?' "

"What's got up your nose?"

"I don't fault what you're doing. It's hard to be in the same town as that filthy little whore. She did this to you. As I see it, you're a paragon of mental health. I admire you for it. But for God's sake admit to a bit of selfishness, enviable selfishness."

"What am I not admitting?"

"You tell me. This would be a rare opportunity for you to distinguish right from righteous . . ."

That's the thing about Koestler. Nick could stay angry if he weren't so spot-on.

". . . or am I being insensitive again?"

NICK'S BEEN AWAY NEARLY THREE WEEKS, the longest he's ever been apart from Charlotte, and he feels it disorienting him. He doesn't like wondering how she is and doesn't like calling to find out. He doesn't like being unable to picture her face, or able to picture it in an aspect—grumpy, transfixed, a-giggle—but unable to put it in motion in his mind. He reminds himself it's silly. If fourteen days has become doable, what makes twenty so tough? And, he wonders, is he also missing Trish? Is he allowed to do that?

He thinks about Sareen. He always looks forward to seeing her. If she wants more from him, he can't feel bad over it right now. It's just the difference from a woman who requires a good scratching up inside, the mammalian need that neither precludes love nor depends upon it—and certainly predates it. The difference from the woman who walked out and took his child but still wants him up in there, still wants him to please find that thing and scratch it some more. Sareen is who she will always be. As Evan said, they make better wives.

Actually what he said was, you can marry a woman who takes it up the ass, but never marry a woman who wants it up the ass. They were sitting at the bar of the Union Square Cafe, eating a late lunch of rare hamburgers after a meeting nearby. People in the States are always plying Brits with beef—it started long ago, before mad cow, and Nick considers it an excellent expression of hospitality. Evan's rap was, the ones who do it to please you will always be doing to please you. The ones who want it wild, dirty, up the old shit chute for their own gratification, they're the ones who eventually start fucking all your friends.

GOING BACK OVER THE THANKSGIVING BREAK, Nick takes off from Kennedy chasing a nor'easter that left town the afternoon before. About ninety minutes out, the old 747-200 starts tossing like a cork. The result is that he doesn't sleep as much as usual and is out of sorts when he gets in to Heathrow. At least Trish is bringing Charlotte over in the early evening, after her swim class. Nick has time to make a few plans, take a long hot soak, and sleep a few hours.

He is up and in his bathrobe, drinking a cup of tea, when the doorbell rings. Charlotte recognizes the flat and recognizes him, but it takes a few minutes before she stops ducking into Trish's shoulder and peering out. At first, it's, I know this guy— he's funny and I like him. After about twenty minutes she stops what she's doing and goes a little vague, her eyes get big, and she reaches for his arms, crying. Charlotte spreads herself across

Nick's chest, her arms around his neck, her wet face buried under his jaw. She isn't crying now, just lying very still so that most of the surface of her is pressed against him.

"Oh sweetie pie, oh darling," he shushes. "It's OK. I missed you too."

"She's had a long and busy day of it, but nothing her Daddy can't fix."

Nick walks around the flat with her, singing "People Get Ready." He'd stopped for vegetable soup and bread at the French grocery. Trish heats the soup and scrambles some eggs while Nick holds Charlotte. He sits her on his lap and puts a hunk of bread—mostly insides, a little crust—into one of her fists, and feeds her soup and eggs.

"She loves her swim class, and she's very good too!"

"What constitutes good?"

"Mummy not letting her drown, and Charlotte splashing a lot."

"Are you a little swimmer, minnow?"

"She's a little bread eater, is what she is."

"She looks well."

"She is well. She picked up a cold last week, but that's passed, and the teething is kind of quiet just now. Have you had a peek?"

"No, but I must when the coast clears."

Nick gives Charlotte a big goofy smile and Charlotte returns it eggily.

"Look at them choppers, girl! How many is it now, six?"

"Seven. See the molar on the bottom left?"

"Oh yes. That's very impressive. You've been hard at work, mademoiselle."

Charlotte stays backed into him as she eats, tuned in to the Mummy and Daddy close time.

"Nick, can we have lunch, maybe tomorrow? Just you and me, so we can go over some things."

"Things?"

"Just plan stuff."

"Sure. I've got three more days. Do you think she can stay overnight?"

"Of course. How's tomorrow?"

"My tomorrows are all for you, little one. All for you."

"Actually, Saturday is better. But why don't you two go out for a date instead?"

Nick drives them back to Islington, then fights the traffic over to West Hampstead. He fancies some drinking with Gorman and Tate, an undemanding evening, a curry and a good night's sleep.

The lads are there and ready to oblige, happy for Nick's good mood, demurely interested in his tales of fatherhood and snapshots of Charlotte, loudly encouraging whatever he will tell about Sareen and his conquest of America. Tate's commentary draws mostly from his intimacy with De Niro's work, Gorman isn't much better, and Nick is pleased with his evening out.


TRISH MEETS HIM NEAR CAMDEN LOCK, at an Italian place. She's got her date manners going, which he always finds touching. Nick has never thought of himself as worldly, since most of his friends are, but he's generally comfortable wherever he goes. Trish, despite the years traveling and years in town, is still a bit of a girl—you can tell she's happy that she knows about things like *vitello tonnato*, and eager to show it. They trade catch-up through the hors d'oeuvres.

"There are two things we need to discuss."

"OK."

"The first is about me. Well, us."

"OK."

"Nick, I'm pregnant. Joe and I . . ."

Nick is flummoxed: the news makes sense, of course, but still it's a trap door opening under his chair. A stunner—not up there with Trish's original lightning bolt, but right now he isn't doing the sums.

"I don't want to be . . . Are you . . ."

"What?"

"I just mean, we didn't use anything, and—"

"I'm sure. Of the timing, and . . ."

"I see. So when . . ."

"It's just around three months. So early June or thereabouts."

"When did you know?"

"For sure? Since about a month."

"Wow, Trish."

"I know. It's weird, right?"

"You must be delighted though."

"We are. You know it doesn't change anything."

"Of course it does. I don't—"

The waiter arrives with squid-ink risottos.

"Sorry, I need a minute to let this sink in. I'm thinking a lot of things, I just need to get them in order."

"God, yes. I know. Charlotte will be a big sister. Joe and I want a large family. And she'll always have the world's best Daddy."

"It's just, everything keeps changing, doesn't it? We're barely into any sort of a rhythm and now it all turns again."

"Yes, well . . ."

"No, it's OK. You're just so full of fucking surprises. Do you make a special effort, or does it come naturally for you?"

"It's a shock, but what . . . I wind up with someone else, more than a year goes by, now we're having a baby."

"Look—"

"I'm the first to say I messed a lot of things up. I messed us up. But this part, now, this is the normal part. Which may not make it any easier for you, but how are you going to look at it? What would be odd is if it weren't happening."

"That's helpful. Thanks for everything. But you'll recall I did have to ask who the father was, which seems to be a bit of a pattern with your offspring. Just how good of a mathematician are you?"

"I know who the father is. I know who the fathers are. I know."

"You said there were two things."

"Yes, I did. What are you planning for Christmas?"

"I'm planning to come home for a few weeks, and to go back right after New Year's. I'm planning to be with my daughter, of course."

"The thing is—I was afraid of this. We're going skiing around then."

"Over Christmas? Over Charlotte's first proper Christmas? Are you mad?"

"We need to talk about this. It's our time too."

"No it's not! It's Christmas! We may be all fucked up. We *are* all fucked up. But some thing, some little part of this, has got to make sense. It's only right, you know? It's not OK, Trish. It's not."

"I wish we could talk about this some other time, but we can't. Plans need to be made. It hasn't been easy for me either. I left. I'm sorry. I left. But here we are, living with this, and we need to make the best of it."

"I don't need to make the best of it."

"Yes you do."

"Why? For Charlotte? Or for you?"

"For everyone."

"How do you dare? Charlotte doesn't ski!"

"We are building our lives here. You go to America. Right. I work and we all work to make it OK. Who says any of it should be easy?"

"So now you're saying I ought not to have gone? You're saying this now?"

"No, I'm not saying that at all. What I am saying is, we've worked together to make it be a good thing, because it's a good thing for you. And if Charlotte and Joe, who loves her and is devoted to her, and I—if we want to go skiing, then that also needs to work. So yes, for Charlotte too."

"You're such a cunt."

"Good. That helps. You need to help."

"And how would you like me to do that?"

"Well, let's think about dates. When will you be here? How early are you intending to come? Should we leave Boxing Day so that you can have Christmas, or a good part of it? Because we need to make our bookings. Or we can leave sooner and come back sooner, before New Year's. We could do that, although I think my other suggestion is better."

Nick knows he won't hit her but he needs to leave now. He

calls for the bill and tells Trish he'll ring her. He walks for fifteen or twenty minutes before realizing he's got to go back for his car. What she's saying isn't unworkable. They could leave Boxing Day and he'd have his Christmas with Charlotte. But it means him bouncing around London for a week when he'd hoped to spend it with her. And she should be spending it with him, being with her Dad every day. That's the truth—he isn't just being selfish, not just selfish. He doesn't expect all their lives to revolve around his arrivals. So he gets to see her the week before, what's a week?

It was the way Trish said it, like they decided and were doing him a favor by letting him adjust to it. God damn her. And she's pregnant. Mathematics? How can she be sure whose kid it is? She talks about normal lives. Doesn't fucking the ex count? Or is that going to stop now too? Didn't sound like it, but who knows, with her?

That burns. Pregnant. So much for any fantasy about her coming back, not that I like admitting to it. Why am I fucked up—because the insides of that girl are so sweet? Because I need to prove I win? How about because every molecule of me wants her back, and now there's no hope.

Unless the kid is mine. And if that's possible, then what about Charlotte? I'd rather lose Trish a thousand times than lose that. Even if it means I've got to believe the most lying, cheating, self-deluding cunt in the history of cunt bitches of the earth.

Believe her? I'm committed to believing her, because she fucks me. And why? Because she likes to. Because it makes it cozy between us. It means she didn't make quite so big of a balls-up. And I do my part: I've still got my tongue up that nectared ass. What was I thinking when we were together and she was traveling half the time? Did I move to New York so I could pretend she didn't leave me? That I'm just away a lot on business?

Now reality intrudes. She's going away, with her real, alive, growing family, and I'm given to know where I stand. Well, I'm Charlotte's father. At least that better be true.

But I know there's something else in Trish and our so unfinished business that makes her keep fucking me. It goes beyond the power trip of presenting herself for me to pray at her altar, and it keeps me hellishly turned on. What is it with her? She's always been this way: that, I know. Who was she doing when she was with me—Joe, Tommy, the towelhead in 4B? To hell with her. The question is, what's my problem?

I should ring up and make sure she's bringing Charlotte tonight. I just don't want to deal with Trish, even with fucking her. Oh crap! What I don't want to deal with is the chance of her not wanting to fuck me. Cool off. See Charlotte. Work out what's going on. Work out the moves forward. Work out what it is I even want.

TRISH IS RELIEVED that Nick has agreed to the Christmas plan, and said congratulations. He's coming round for Charlotte. Is what she's done so wrong if it ends up working, for everyone involved?

Charlotte is wearing a pink and green dress and green tights, with a flowered clip in her hair. She knows she's beautiful, and knows she's going out on some kind of a spree. When she's sees it's with Daddy, she writhes ecstatically, like a squirt of batter hitting the fryer.

In the car, Nick puts on the Impressions CD. When

"Woman's Got Soul" comes up they bop along. Nick takes them to a sit-down fish and chips restaurant in Kensington. He orders a pint of bitter, prawn cocktail, cod and chips and peas. Charlotte drinks milk from her sippy cup. After an open-minded attempt she passes on the prawns but endorses the buttered brown bread. They sit at an angle to each other, Charlotte in a wooden high chair with a view of the room. She greets everyone, watches everyone pass, studies every plate, comments on everything. She wants Nick's full attention, and makes sure she keeps it, through eye contact and by throwing "Da" into every bit of chatter. She's OK with the cod but loves the mushy peas and chips and tartar sauce: an interesting landscape takes form on the tray of the high chair. Nick pulls her sleeves up but she's got peas mashed into her hair. At some point the clip comes off. She eats her way up chip after chip, singing and smiling raucously. When she's finished, she slunks down in her chair, with the look of a pensioner remembering the war. Her face reddens with effort.

"Oh good. You're running a full-service operation."

Nick debates changing her at the restaurant, but they're near enough to Kentish Town. They share a quick apple crumble, then mop up, pay up, and drive back. Nick loves to change her: seeing her beautiful body, and her comfort in him, seeing that she runs well, making raspberries into her belly. Nick sings to her and compliments her work. He kisses her hands and snuggles his face into hers and gets her giggle going.

"So many peas in your coiffure, mademoiselle."

He runs a bath and puts her in. It's been a few months since they've done this together, another way to see how much control she's gained over her world. Charlotte loves to be in the tub with these half-familiar, under-explored toys. Nick kneels beside her, watching her become engrossed in the colors and characters, pushing them away and catching them back, telling them about the world in her sing-song.

"Beshau. Dyp Dyp."

The sounds have syntax, if not vocabulary.

"Dis." She holds up Po for him to see. "Po."

"Very good, little one. Who's this?" He holds up Tinky Winky.

"Po!"

"OK, a deeper truth!"

Charlotte laughs, eyes crinkling like a pirate, mouth open and flashing her choppers. Nick washes and rinses her hair. Charlotte sits very still, ballerina posture, receiving her beauty treatment.

"Up and out!" Nick dries, combs and diapers her, puts the pink and green dress back on, the green tights, laces the white shoes.

When Nick drops her off, he explains, "We had a bath. It was that or bring you back a pea-head."

"You had a bath with Daddy?"

"Da." Charlotte smiles.

"I'm glad. You two had fun."

"We had big fun. Tomorrow evening?"

"We'll be in the country, so I'll bring her over on our way back. Around five?"

"Whenever you say."

"Are you going to sleep over at Daddy's tomorrow?"

Charlotte snuggles into Mummy, happy with the world and mostly Trish's shoulder.

———

NICK MEETS JOHNNY FOR DINNER at San Lorenzo. She's been back in Canada for a month and is going to spend the holidays hiking in Peru. She's tweaked: gaunt, smoking non-stop, changing subjects incoherently. Nick knows he ought to show some enthusiasm. She's been so devoted to him. Does she have any plans for herself? What could that possibly mean in Johnny's case? She's too old to do Condé Nast or a course at Sotheby's. She has no need to work, or interest in it. For Nick the issue with Johnny has always been her availability to him. She prides herself on being an excellent friend. Except when family drama rears up, or when there's a man on the scene, and Nick gets less of her. Now he has hardly noticed Johnny in his despair over Trish, hardly noticed how close she is to him, that he has accomplished what had been his goal in life since forever. He knows that it might never have happened under other circumstances. But it occurred, largely from Johnny's empathy—at least it wasn't pity or charity—and in part from the shock of his sudden lack of pursuit. The gap between them had been filled for so long by Nick's desire that its dispersion created an instability And that vacuum has sucked Johnny toward him: instability, as any banker knows, equals opportunity. He appreciates the gift he's been given, and its ironies, appreciates Johnny's goodness, and is moved by her love.

But it bears no relation to the blind twisted longing that walked him around London one hundred times, broke bottles, jacked him off, and bored Tommy and Koestler since their teens. All that was not this, and in the midst of the new real pain he can hardly celebrate its departure.

"Have you taken some sort of drug?" Nick asks.

"No, why?"

"You're off, agitated. What is it, darling?"

"Bad few days. I stink from smoke, I'm constipated. I cut myself in the kitchen making soup last night."

"I'd rather hear about the source than the symptoms, if you don't mind."

"Can't talk, OK? But how are you? Don't look well yourself, you know."

Nick dislikes her avoidance, and that he can't dump his suffering onto someone whose eyes are jumping around like this. He wants a Let's Cuddle Me session, and resents not getting it.

"Just the broken home blues. But Charlotte is in top form. That's what matters."

"Hey, can we go dancing tonight? Would you mind?"

"Where?"

"There's a club in Putney, very tatty but it's all seventies soul music. Just your sort of thing. And you're bound to know people there."

"We could use a bit of a session, couldn't we? But not too late. I've got a match in the country tomorrow and I'll be hopeless enough as it is."

They down two bottles of overpriced Tuscan white, eat a little of what they've ordered, and drive to Putney. Nick doesn't know anyone, but probably several older siblings of these fresh beauties. Johnny dances epileptically. Nick hears some beloved cuts—"Be Thankful for What You've Got," "South African Man," "Wicky Wacky." He takes Johnny back to Campden Hill Square. She wants him to come in. She's acting bratty, almost like she wants him to smack her. Johnny is still twitching like a pillhead as she lets herself in.

———

HE DRIVES OUT TO THE MATCH WITH TOMMY, plays as well as he ever does—offering a lot of hustle, and the absence of mistakes, and not much else. He leaves right after, races back to town and bathes. Trish and Charlotte are at his door just after six. Joe waves from the Jaguar.

"Bye-bye. Bye-bye, Ja."

Nick kisses Charlotte. So he's "Ja." Better Ja than Da.

"I'll stay a bit, if that's all right, to get her settled. We're out to dinner later."

Nick lets them in and walks to the car.

"Joe. Congratulations."

"Thank you. We're very excited."

"I know it's going to be great. For both of you, and Charlotte getting a sister or brother. Good luck with it."

Joe clasps the offered hand.

Inside, Charlotte is cruising around a table onto which Trish has spilled a bag of toys. Nick goes to make tea and Trish follows.

"We've got dinner at nine, so I thought we'd feed Charlotte and hang out with her, put her to bed if she's ready. We're not up to anything tomorrow, so you can do whatever works for you."

Trish is close to him in the small kitchen. Her smell, as usual, is unendurable, womanly wonder, honey and wet earth. Charlotte has crawled into the doorway. She sits quietly and studies them—Trish leaning against the counter, Nick making the tea.

"She loves you so much. She's a Daddy's girl."

"I certainly hope so. Are you? Are you a Daddy's girl? There are worse things, I promise you."

Dinner is take-out pizza and some microwaved carrots.

Charlotte points an index finger at each little square of pizza, sticks the tip into the cheese, and directs it to her mouth, sometimes with success. Nick eats his pizza. Trish joins him in a glass of red. Everything she wants to say—this is hard, we'll muddle through, what counts is our love for her—is too corny, and she knows that Nick knows anyway.

What she says is, "It's funny—or not, considering that we share the most important thing in the world. But it's funny, how you and I have gotten to know each other over the last year or so. Backwards business, yeah?"

"To backwards business." Nick raises his glass. Trish can hear the steel in his voice.

They play on the carpet, get Charlotte changed for bed. She is busy introducing the Kentish Town dolls and stuffed animals to Baby and Bunny, who have come with her from home. She gnaws each in turn. Trish gives her a bottle and lays her into the crib.

"Night night, Charlotte. Night night, Da." She kisses his cheek and leaves.

Charlotte wakes up at two-thirty. Nick goes in to get her. He wonders if he's moved too soon, but she's upset and he doesn't want to let it spiral. She's indignant, seeing that it's him. You're the fun guy. Where the hell is Mummy?

"It's OK, it's OK," he whispers, and tries to sing some of their songs while putting a bottle together by the light of the open refrigerator. The bottle from Da is an insult, bordering on an outrage, and Charlotte starts to wail. Nick can see she's OK: no fever, no congestion, belly's fine. Just night time, and no Mama. He isn't going to ring Trish, although he knows he can. It isn't that he'd be admitting he can't handle it—of course he can't; this howl only wants one thing. But she'll be fine. They'll do this together. After about half an hour of escalating bloody murder, Charlotte plateaus. He tries the bottle again, and on the fourth gentle attempt she accepts it.

"Get it where you can, little one, and how you can."

She sucks steadily, still complaining some, but her body untenses and she starts to ease into him in the usual way. He carries her to his room and makes a wall of pillows on one side of the bed. He takes the bottle from his groggy froggy and lays her down. Nick stretches out on the other side and watches her until she's asleep—on her back, one leg over a pillow, arms out to the sides, like a drunken caliph. He stays propped up on an elbow for about an hour, looking at his child: her breathing; her hands, closed but not clenched; her long lashes and clever brow. Whatever got me to this moment, right here, tonight, now, was worth it. Thank you, God. And he thinks, how strange that I have helped to make this girl. She looks like me. There are things we do together, private glances and jokes that are more complex and complicitous than any I have ever shared with anyone. Because of genetic circuitry that years could not wire as we two have been wired. And just as she is blood, also she is other.

I am male and have spent my life in thrall to women. Lust and wonder and regret are the commodities on my exchange, and I understand them less than ever. But here is one, a prototype female, my girl. My DNA in a woman. Will I understand her? I love her as I love myself.

He remembers, a few days after Charlotte was born, hearing Prince's "I Would Die 4 U" on the radio. It was one of his favorite songs but he heard it differently now. Die for you? That's the least of it. Dying is easy. I would never exist, for you to exist. I would kill without consideration. But how do I live for you? What do I do to make you happy and strong, to give you access to your buccaneer heart? How do I do this job that I have never done, and do it better than it was done for me, and how do I do it for a girl, when girls are the very thing I know least? Love most and know least. Trish, for all her faults, is a good and strong person, and maybe in her way a happy one. Her love comes with handles. She knows what to do for you, like she's already read and forgotten the instruction manual. Mine is an ocean, but it doesn't come with charts, or even a dinghy. Charlotte, on the contrary, is perfectly equipped. She knows who Mummy and Daddy are, and she knows what we're for. We're to love her. She reaches out or pulls away, laughs or cries, and draws a pure line between desire and action. But I can't expect her to teach me. That's not her job, it's mine.

He's sleepy, and glad to be. He wants to be bright and full of fun for Charlotte when she wakes.


NEW YORK, skidding out of its Thanksgiving turn, tears wildly toward Christmas. Except for Nick, who's joined too recently, everyone at the office is in febrile suspense over what the bonuses will be. People shop, make holiday plans, go to parties—and still try to move their deals along. Half the derelicts who usually sell *The Street News* are done up in ratty Santa suits, ringing bells outside the department stores. Only Sareen is as she was before, and happy to have Nick back.

He mulls over what to do for the week when Charlotte will be in Zermatt. Should he stay home or go somewhere himself? And does he feel like asking Sareen along? He wants to be in London for Charlotte's return, but he doesn't want to deal with Sareen there. He doesn't need his worlds to meet, if these can even be said to constitute his worlds. Sareen belongs in the imaginary city, not Kentish Town.

He proposes that she meet him somewhere. He's always wanted to see Naples and thereabouts. It isn't skiing—too weird with Charlotte and Trish a few Alps over—or risking a beach at this time of year. They could meet in Italy. She would fly in and out of Rome. They'd take the train down, see Pompeii, maybe Capri, surely Positano. Sareen is up for all of it.

Bonus day comes. It's only the announcement: the checks don't get cut until the new year. People are fairly happy, and Evan is happier than most. Nick is startled to find himself with a healthy taste, after less than three months of work. So everyone is in good spirits at the Christmas parties.

Sareen is loving and open, not taxing them with expectations. Or is that just how he wants to see it? They've known each other for as long as he and Trish did when they got married. No comparisons, please. For starters, this one likes her parents, which may be why she's so much less of a piece of work. Is that why it still doesn't matter to him? Nick knows how lucky he is. He just doesn't really care. Would he ever have been like this, before the suffering of the last year schooled him?

Sareen thinks more clearly than she lets on. Is she falling in love? There is stuff going on here that she can't explain or control. But she understands that intricate claims lie upon this man. She isn't entirely sure of their nature or who, other than Charlotte, lays them. So she will wait, watch, and hope. She can be patient. But Nick has to offer some of his soul for her to offer hers.

As it turns out, Venice has the best weather in Italy over Christmas, picking up some of the persistent high pressure that gives the Alps a legendary season. Naples is caught in a corresponding low. Battered by a persistent damp wind, Naples and the south remain overcast throughout the holidays. But Nick and Sareen never get there, owing to climatic change elsewhere.


DECEMBER 10 IS CHARLOTTE'S FIRST BIRTHDAY, and it hurts Nick to be away. He can't justify a trip, on several levels: it's the middle of the week; he was just back and will be back again a week from now; it's an important time to be among his new colleagues. Still, all he feels is guilty, that he's falling short.

Charlotte is spending her birthday with Trish and Joe. The party will be on Saturday, when Maggie's family will celebrate with them, along with Trish's parents, and Simon and Emily, Charlotte's friends from her play group. Nick has left his present for her: a stroller that she can walk behind and push, with a doll wearing a yellow sweater that says "Mummy's girl," and a matching sweater in Charlotte's size that says "Daddy's girl." Nick is in the office at one that day when Trish calls. Nick talks to Charlotte. She loves telephones. They put him on the speaker so that he can join in "Happy Birthday" when the chocolate cake, Charlotte's first, is presented. She loves it, takes a bath in it, and Trish videotapes the whole thing for Nick to see. He goes out to lunch in a sorrowful mood and walks around midtown by himself. When Sareen asks about it that night she gets a shrug, followed by an uncommunicative fucking.

On Saturday Nick plays football in Riverside Park, a regular game with Italian bankers and Ghanaian taxi drivers. When he picks up his shirt, he finds a message on his cell phone.

"Nick, it's Trish. I don't know if you can hear this, it's pretty noisy here. Listen—don't worry, everything's OK, I think. We're at St. Hilda's, the hospital. I didn't see how it happened, but Maggie's youngest boy Jackson was playing with Charlotte, and somehow she ate a peanut from a bowl of nuts I put out. I must be a fucking idiot, but anyhow it went down the wrong way, and according to the doctor, she aspirated it, which is what they call it when you inhale something you shouldn't. It's not like she was choking or anything—"

The message stops. New message.

"Sorry, I'm back, I think it lost me. Anyway, so she inhaled this peanut, which I saw as it was happening, but it seemed like, 'oh, she's fine.' But then she didn't look right to me, so we called the pediatrician, who said to bring her in.

"They want to keep her here to see whether or not they need to do anything. They took an X-ray. There's a fucking peanut in her right lung. Everyone says she'll be fine, but I guess there's a risk of pneumonia, so they're going to keep an eye on her. They don't know whether they'll need to get it out or not, but they'll let us know. They're going to let me stay over with her, so I'll be here at the hospital. I don't know the number but I'll leave it for you, or you can try me on my mobile. I'm such a fucking idiot. OK, bye."

Nick calls Trish on her cell phone, but he can't get through. He leaves a message that he's making arrangements and will be there in the morning. In the cab back to his apartment he listens to Trish's messages again, twice, through all the blood pounding in his head. It sounds OK. Really, it sounds OK. He leaves a message for Sareen and calls a doctor friend of Evan's.

The phone rings while Nick is in the shower, trying to make the eight o'clock BA flight. It's the doctor, Marcussen. Nick is grateful. Dr. Marcussen is unrushed and reassuring. Normal childhood drama, happens more than you think, if they're on top of it there's not much chance of anything bad happening. In the car to the airport Trish gets Nick.

"What's going on?"

"She's fine. I'm an idiot, but Charlotte is fine."

"What do they say?"

"They saw it. It's a peanut, you know? They don't see any sign of pneumonia, which is what the risk is from something like this. Aspiration pneumonia. Apparently it happens all the time."

"How is she? Who's with her now?"

"Maggie and Joe. She's fine, you know—another place to check out, more people to smile at. She isn't in pain or anything, probably just wondering at the kerfuffle. Maybe she thinks it's a part of the birthday."

"So what are the risks?"

"As I follow it, the risk is of the peanut making her get an infection, which would be the pneumonia. And I guess that would be bad, quite bad in a small child. So they make sure that isn't happening, and then they decide whether to take it out or not. I think that's right."

"And if they need to take it out, then what?"

"Stick a tube down. It's not surgery or anything. They make her sleepy, you know—"

"When will they decide what to do about it?"

"I don't know. When they decide. Right now they're just watching it. Look, Nick, I think it's—I totally understand you wanting to be here, and if it were at all—I mean, they may not do anything. If I were you, I'd stay handy and book a flight for tomorrow just in case. I'll call at every turn."

"Can I talk to her? Are you near her?"

"No, but I'll ring you back from in the room. I'm not saying don't come. It's just that I know how hard it is, and I don't think there's any point, not for her at least, on any level. She's fine."

"Bloody hell, Trish, you're telling me everything, right?"

"I'm telling you absolutely everything. I could never take it upon myself to do anything else. You know that."

"Yes."

"I'll call you back from the room. Listen, twenty years ago people didn't run to the hospital every time somebody sucked down a nut. You went if you were sick, and she's not sick. I swear it."

"OK. Ring me back."

Trish hangs up as Nick is passing La Guardia. She calls back at the start of the Van Wyck.

"I have somebody for you!"

"Sha Sha?"

"Da! Da dis!"

"Nick? She's got the biggest smile but— No, dearest, it's a phone, not a hammer. Talk. Talk to Da. OK, Nick, say something."

Nick sings the start of "Red, Red Robin" and a satellite bounces back the sound of his love, cooing along with him.

"She seems like herself, doesn't she?" Nick asks.

"I'm telling you. You run back and forth so much. If it will make you feel the tiniest bit better, come over. But you wouldn't get on a plane for chicken pox, and that would be a lot harder on her."

"OK, look. I'm almost there, so I'm going to get to Kennedy, check my flight, and I'll see how the rest of the weekend looks for seating. And then I'm going to have a beer and decide."

"That sounds right, whatever you do."

"OK. I'll call back."

Nick checks that there is availability on flights. He's going back in six days, and really ought to be around that week. It's all nonsense if Charlotte is in trouble, or if Trish needs him there, but that's not what he's hearing. If Trish is right in her information, then she's right in her advice. And a mother knows. She would see it if Charlotte didn't seem right, and she would tell him, and he would hear it in her voice. And she would never mislead him on something like this. He believes that. What about Charlotte? She doesn't know anything is wrong, and her Mummy is right there with her. So it's back to the city for tonight.

But as soon as Nick gets in the taxi he doesn't feel right. The ride is eternal. Sareen is at work, his work friends are in their pre-holiday weekends, and Nick doesn't want to be among them now anyway.

The last time he spoke to Trish it was midnight there. What were they all doing, up at midnight, if everything's fine? Has he got the straight story? Yes, what else could it be? But in any case, there's no way he can phone back until their morning. Hospitals rise early, so, what, 2:00 A.M. his time? It's clear to him now that he should have gone, if only for his sanity. He watches a movie, goes out for some sushi and manages to eat too much, sucking down piece after piece as his mind dances.

At two, he calls. Dialing, he recognizes that the smothering knot is the same as the one when she left him. Here he is, desperate for her news again. May this time turn out better, that's all.

"Trish!"

"Hi. It's late, right?"

"So?"

"She slept well, better than me. We're playing and waiting for breakfast. It's Daddy!"

"Eeeeh!" It's her reaching sound.

"Hi, precious, how are you? It's your Da."

"Da Da! Mmm."

"Are you waiting for breakfast with Mummy?"

"Mm. Ma!"

"You're witty, all right. OK, you one-year-old, pass me ba—"

"Hello again. Well, you hear it for yourself."

"Anything of note at all?"

"Just a peanut in her lung. A touch of fever."

"What?"

"They say it's normal, they're not concerned. Don't you be."

"What exactly do they say? Do they think it's the start of something?"

"The doctors are supposed to turn up soon, on their morning rounds. I'll know more then, or maybe later, if there is more."

"Meaning? What is the 'it' that they would do, if they did it? Help me out."

"I told you, a tube. It's called a bronchoscopy. Get her groggy, have a look, possibly do a little hoovering. Nick, no one here is acting very concerned, and I don't think I'm just being coddled. Go to bed. Call me when you wake up."

"Trish, promise you'll phone with any news. I don't care if you wake me up ten times. I'll be able to sleep if I know you'll call me."

"OK."

"You'd want me to do the same for you. And I would."

"It's true. Both. Nick? Go to sleep. Our baby is fine."

Sareen arrives just before three. Nick tells her the full version, beyond the news flash he'd given her at work. They go to bed and Nick falls quickly and fitfully asleep. He wakes at six-thirty. The phone has not rung. He calls Trish on the mobile, and gets her.

"No news. Lots of friendly faces, still some fever. About the same, a degree. Everyone says they'll let us know. We're running out of things to do here, but that's our only worry at the moment. We're just hanging around."

"Trish, you sound different. How concerned are you, really?"

"I'm concerned. It's a long stretch, Charlotte's restless. I know it's good that no one thinks we're important. I'd rather be unimportant in this place. But I want her home and to have everything be OK."

"Would it help if I was there for you?"

"I'm holding up. I took a break this morning, and I'll go out and get some lunch when Mum comes. I'll call. You know."

"I'm thinking about you two."

"You're sweet."

Is it just selfishness, not getting on a plane, or would getting on the plane be the selfishness? Now his main fear is that he'll be over the ocean when there's news to hear, or perhaps to act upon, decisions to make. Nick calls Grace and Marcus to let them know. Grace shows no alarm. She says she'll call right away, not to be a further burden, just to see if they can be of some help. Nick thanks her and urges them to use the flat in Kentish Town if they come in.

Grace says, "I know this is probably the hardest on you, but you're being very wise to listen to Trish. Mothers do know, you know."

Nick spends the day around the flat. He tells Sareen she should sleep, but she gets up and goes out to shop for breakfast.

She cooks steak and eggs, massages Nick—scalp, neck, back and legs—and then administers an unadorned closing blow job. He's amazed and fairly appalled that he gets with it, but he can't ignore his dick in her mouth. It helps. Can you fall in love with someone for taking perfect care of you, instead of for putting you on the rack?

Trish calls at eleven. "They've just been waiting, it turns out, for the ace tube-man to show up. They're going to do it now. He's very nice. He says it could take about ninety minutes but might go longer, what with getting down to the room and recovery and so on. He says it's straightforward. We should be going home in the morning."

"Is that the best thing? Are there other options?"

"They seem very clear on this."

"Will you be with her?"

"No, damn. They're giving her a general, because of her age. I'll be with her when she goes under, and when she comes out of it. I asked. They won't let me."

"Who's there?"

"Mum and Dad, Grace and Marcus. It was lovely of them to come. Charlotte will think this was the best party ever."

"Are they in the way?"

"No, they're darlings. They phoned, and I asked them to come."

"Is Joe there with you?"

"Yes, of course."

"I'm glad. I'm sorry I'm not there."

"I wish you were. I mean, I'm glad you listened to me, but for right now—she's our girl."

"Trish, I always knew you were the strongest woman on the planet. Charlotte has the greatest mum ever."

"Don't fret. I'll call at once."

The first two hours are tough but the third is in its own category. Then Trish calls at two-twenty, New York time. Charlotte is foggy and very uncomfortable, but she's fine. They got the peanut. They'll be home by lunch time Monday.

Sareen leads Nick to the bedroom, pulls down the blackout shades, and tucks him in with a Xanax and a big glass of water.

"I'll be here. Try to sleep."

Nick can't see it happening but he obeys, and doesn't wake until evening.


IT'S TRUE. Charlotte is OK. She has a fairly miserable night and goes home at noon, sore-throated and short-tempered. A fuss is made and she recovers quickly. By Wednesday she's coming to the phone for Nick. It's been a fever dream for him, the unreality of being off in New York and hearing about it all, but now Nick starts to think it through.

His baby in hospital, his baby under a general anesthetic: they were so blessed that it had gone well. But he's enraged over how Trish handled things. He should have been there. He blames himself entirely for not getting on that Saturday flight. He was too easily convinced, mostly out of a laughable calculus that his not going somehow created the reality that Charlotte was not in peril. Trish must have believed that too. But Trish, Trish and Joe, were happy to handle it on their own. That, rock bottom, was what happened, and he was happy to allow it.

Is he grateful to Joe for loving Charlotte? How does he know if Joe loves Charlotte, or just loves being perfect, the perfect stepdad? Pushing the stroller around Islington, does he even tell people? Yes, he would. That's his triumph and his achievement, his pride. And Charlotte loves him like a daddy. Fuck Trish's PR, he's her daddy fifty times more hours a month than I am. Well, lucky girl, she has two.

Just like Mum. Who, lest we forget, is the person at fault here. When you take responsibility for a life, you are totally responsible, so when you fuck up you are totally at fault. And now she's pregnant, and so Charlotte, along with her sore throat and bumpy brush with life experience, will get to learn about sharing Mum with someone new. Trish likes double action in babies as well as boys. But can Trish hope to love them the same? The hand-me-down and the rightful prince or princess? Joe can't, and no fault there. But Charlotte, whose life is weird enough as it is, goes from being the sole shining star of three skies to the shining star of one, the overcast one at that. Just deal with it, little girl. Could Trish not have waited a year or two? That's her definition of responsibility. Get knocked up. Let your baby eat peanuts. Fuck your ex when the mood strikes.

At least he's past wondering if Charlotte is his. Not because she looks like him, and nothing like Joe. It's that bigger questions, life-and-death stuff, have come and gone. He's just over it. Charlotte, he knows, laid her cosmic claim to him. And kid number two? Put that one to rest while you're at it. Might it be a Clifford? Trish, in the brutal logic of her math, doesn't care. Two kids, two cocks, two proud papas. Only a pedant would ask her to connect the dots. It's not an issue for her. Pretty young mum, handsome successful husband, well-trained ex. Two beauties to walk in the park. Why should she care?

NICK CANCELS THE ITALY TRIP. He explains to Sareen that he wants to spend the time with Charlotte. She is more disappointed than

147

she says, and he can see it. But she understands. They'll go somewhere warm in February. He wants to be all there, undivided. Sareen—wow, has she ever come through for him.

They go to bed and Nick wraps himself around her. He kisses Sareen's forehead and thanks her. He wants to be with her, even if he's too fucked up to tell her now and have it mean what it needs to mean. So he's careful to say only what he's certain is true: I owe you so much; you are a blessing; I want us to be together; hang with me through all this bullshit.

Nick can feel her distance. He turns on the light and sits up. "Let's talk."

"OK. What?"

"That didn't come out right."

Sareen crosses her legs and sits facing him, trying not to look as hurt as she feels, because he doesn't have the right to see it now. Nick can't help registering how lovely she is, all neck and ankles, a thoroughbred with a breaking heart.

"I love you. You're the most beautiful person, inside and outside, that I've ever known. I want to take care of you, the way you took care of me. And right now I would like to peel those ridiculous legs apart, and spend a month drinking you. I want to make promises. But the least I can do is explain, even if you know this already, why I won't make those promises tonight.

"I did this once before and I fucked up. It fucked me up. You know all that. Well and truly, you know it. I hope the day comes when I'm not fucked up, and I'm not so bitter, and my love is worth giving to you. Whatever you do with it, I'll understand. Just please, Sareen, don't go anywhere. I'm a good person. But I've got to be careful, or else I'll have another stupid crime to show for my good intentions."

She can't look at him. How pompous, how presumptuous! It's not enough. Maybe she isn't being fair, but it's not enough. She knows he can feel it in her body. Sareen turns out the light. She turns over and pulls him up behind her on the bed. She doesn't want him to see it on her face.

# PART THREE

ick dreads being in London and seeing the people he loves. Except for Charlotte, he isn't sure he wants to figure in their lives, either not any more, or not for the time being. He feels bashful about seeing his daughter. How much of that is shame that he didn't come, how much a sense that she will be different after her experience? What is he imagining, Marlene Dietrich in snap-up pants?

Nick goes straight to Islington from the airport. It's Friday. Joe must be at work. What he feels weird about is Trish: how did that only occur to him now, when it's always about her? She looks tired, but adorable. Nick has felt so many things, so many bad things these last few days. But they can see a change in each other, a recognition of purpose, joined like their DNA. It's all about protecting the kid and loving her, isn't it? They've known it since those strips turned blue in the loo in West Hampstead, so how can it be new? Because it is—not the truth, not the depth of the truth, but the flavor of the truth, a taste of something they don't need to discuss. It isn't a particularly good taste, but it's a timeless one, of the value of the thing. And it passes in a second.

"Hi, Trish."

"How was the flight?"

"Like they all are."

"Come up. She's in mid-nap. A busy morning with the play group."

"So she's back in action one hundred percent."

"She was never out of it."

Nick's eyebrow rises.

"No, it was just a very awkward weekend, and a foul Sunday. That's all ages ago, on her scale."

"I suppose. And how was it for you, really?"

"It was rough at moments. The time she was up in surgery was the worst of course, but I'm sure that was worse for you, sitting an ocean away and waiting for the phone to ring."

"You handled the whole thing brilliantly. I know about the A Levels and flight-attendant school, but you must have slipped in a few years at the Emma Peel Academy."

"No, just the 'hysterical mum pretending she's together' evening class. If I seem capable of anything, I guess the act is working."

"You know how you are. You know I know."

"I can be a fairly handy thing. But you're a man, so of course you're impressed. You're all the same—emotional, over-reacting, self-doubting, self-congratulating. We ponder less and get on with it more. I wasn't nearly as upset as you think, because I was busy getting on with it."

Nick wants to kiss her, and Trish may want to be kissed. But is it on, in Joe's house? And it strikes him that the first moves are always hers—have to be. Trish opens a window. Sideways on, he sees the convexity of her tummy where the tee shirt rides up. That beloved lychee of a belly button, already getting pushed out by the growing child. How sexy. Fuck, she's showing.

"She's got this new thing. You'll see." Trish seats herself on the Persian rug in front of Nick. He puts his hand in the thickness of her hair. Trish does that feline turn of her neck to both acknowledge and decline the gesture.

"I'm so rude. Can I get you something? A beer?"

They are saved by the irate cry of a waking toddler. They go up to Charlotte's room. She's standing in her crib, hair tousled, jaw set in Churchillian resolve. She's wearing jeans and a tee shirt, like her mother.

"You two must stop traffic."

"Well, peanuts, anyway. Come out, flower. Look who's here."

Charlotte knows, but Trish's words uncork the bottle of joy and expectation.

"Da! Da Da!"

Nick takes her from Trish and hugs and kisses her. Charlotte nuzzles him back.

"Would you like to change her nappy?"

"Of course I would."

"I'll go make us some, what, coffee?"

Charlotte watches Trish leave and Nick stay. She whinges a bit on the changing table, but Nick is quick to get her done and downstairs. Trish offers Charlotte a biscuit. She pulls herself up off the floor, using the side of the cocktail table, and cruises around to Trish.

"She's good at that, isn't she?"

"She's getting good at all sorts of things. Wait."

Charlotte chews, waving her biscuit around in jerky celebration.

"Yum?"

She smiles her toothiest Daddy smile, and squeaks, "Dish dow! Dish dow!"

"Dish dow," Nick answers. "You're absolutely right."

Trish rolls in Nick's birthday present. Charlotte's baby has taken over possession of the stroller. "It's Baby! And she's in your present from Daddy. From Daddy, Charlotte."

"Bebeh!" Charlotte reaches over for the stroller from the cocktail table, passing herself from one to the other with a careful confidence. She pushes Baby in the stroller, lurching along, balanced on the handles. When she gets to the shadows of the landing she leans over to pat Baby, kisses it on the head, turns around and comes back, resolute.

"So what are you doing over the holidays?" asks Trish.

"What are your plans now?"

"As before. We leave for Zermatt on Boxing Day, back on the third. Will you still be here then?"

"I don't know. I guess with what happened, I imagined . . ."

"I'm sorry. If you—"

"No, I can see she's perfectly fine. I shouldn't have assumed . . . I should have asked."

"I'm sorry if you changed your plans."

"It's not a problem. We'll spend time this week, I'll see some people. I expect I'll be here for a day or two when you get back."

"I know it's not ideal, Nick."

"A lot is not ideal, but a lot is. Look at Thomasina the Tank Engine there."

"She's something, yeah?"

"So—this week?"

"We're wide open. Whatever you fancy."

"What are you up to tomorrow?"

"Joe and I are due in the country for dinner and overnight. If I come by late morning we can spend the day. She can stay over with you, but let's make sure she's comfortable with it, since getting back would be tricky for us. She's been a bit clingy since the whole business."

"Then let's try for sleeping over on Sunday."

"Yes, any time. It's just a matter of reading her mood. And it's only that tomorrow night we're away, so . . ."

"What is she up to now?"

"Why don't you take her out for a walk. Walk with Daddy?" Charlotte smiles. "Walk with Daddy!"


NICK IS TIRED and he'd like a bath, but he thinks he'll crash if he does that. So he goes to collect his car and calls Tommy for dinner, and Johnny for dinner on Saturday. Lining up the old guard. And in that spirit he goes by the Cooper's Arms to find Gorman and Tate. Halfway down his first pint, Gorman appears, looking done in.

"My God, it's Mr. Clifford."

"Gorman, how are you keeping?"

"I've been better. I'll get us some beers and come over."

Gorman worked at Glaxo in the area of sales forecasting. He has been defenestrated in a nothing-personal exercise of analyst pleasing and right-sizing. This compounds his pre-existing woes: an ailing mother-in-law, a withdrawn wife.

"And where's Tate? He's usually first in."

"Young Master Tate is in the Seychelles."

"Really!"

"Love has blossomed. He sold her a Discovery and she took his heart in the bargain."

"And now they're bronzing in paradise. What's she like?"

"Two kids, divorced. Well looked after by the ex, a City man of considerable means."

"Have you had a sighting?"

"Looks good for, I'd say, early forties. I can only imagine what our boy subjects it to, and how grateful it must be. Looks like a goer. Six gin and Bitter Lemons in ninety minutes. Played with his hair the whole time."

"Have they got a future?"

"Oh, I don't think so. He's down-market for her, and she'll start looking to move the other way."

"Tate see it like that?"

"Sure. She acts like she's dating a pop star. You can picture it, can't you?"

"Well jolly good for Tate. How's it looking for you?"

"Fuck, I don't know. Just don't get re-engineered at Christmas is my only advice. After New Year's I'll send out the CVs, lunch around the brethren, and see what I can scare up."

"Was it a blow? Stupid question. I just mean—"

"I know. Yes and no. No, I don't care, in the big ways. My friends are my friends. The work wasn't particularly interesting any more. Yes, because I doubt that what I'll get will come close. I'll get something, but it won't match what I had. And I'm sorry, but after twelve years of hard work, only moderate cynicism, and daily contact, I came to see things a bit the Glaxo way. 'We're better because,' 'A corporation is its people.' Minus whomever we need to shoot to make a number we should have known not to promise in the first place. After a dozen top reviews and division and discretionary bonuses, it's hard to appreciate the thoughtfulness of free counseling sessions and career-planning seminars. I had a fucking career plan. Do good work for Glaxo and keep the wolf from my door."

"They should call it a career Plan B seminar."

Gorman coughs beer up his nose in appreciation.

"So—on a scale of one to ten?"

"I'm a three. I can't lie to you."

"Send me a CV, OK? And a note with some idea of the range."

Gorman nods and Nick goes for his round.

HE DRIVES DOWN TO LANGTON STREET, where Belinda is belaboring dinner. Oysters in a cream and Pernod sauce that looks like baby throw-up, veal roast in a crust with *pommes purées*, a salad with beets and slivered hazelnuts that tastes like ice water. Tommy compensates with stunning wines. It's just the three of them at the trestle table in the kitchen, very cozy. Then Belinda disappears and Tommy breaks out the Armagnac and Upmann No. 2s. Perhaps because with Tommy he can let it, Nick feels his mood sink. The world, he knows, awaits him—his daughter, London, then Sareen. But it feels like he's the one waiting, in airports, in Kentish Town, in New York. For what? He knew better, even before Trish got pregnant again. That's why he went to New York, to act rather than be acted upon. It's more than the week in London that feels like limbo, it's everything.

"It'll be good fun. We'll go out, behave badly."

"Thanks."

"Maybe we should go up to Scotland. My brother's staging a disgusting scene. Not that all of Scotland isn't a disgusting scene that week."

"Do I need to decide?"

"Never. If the rooms are taken we'll just throw you in with some virgins."

Nick drives home carefully, with what he's had to drink. He's been wanting a hot bath all day, but he throws off his clothes and goes to bed.


HE RISES, RUNS AND BATHES, unable to shake his foul mood. The day is fine. Trish and Charlotte arrive and they drive out to a petting zoo in Windsor. Charlotte laughs and blushes and smooches at the sheep and llamas. Back in Kentish Town she's still napping as they carry her in from the car.

"She'll be up soon. I'll make us some tea."

Trish heads down to the kitchen. Nick sits in the rocker watching Charlotte sleep. What was that? An apology for not fucking him? An admission that she wants to and is sorry they can't? Nick looks at the painting of cows in a field as he considers just how shameful he is. She's been on his mind for weeks, and certainly each of the past twenty-four hours. He's still so possessed. How can he give her this power over him? How can he use his darling Charlotte as a pretext for the taking of the sacrament? Breathing her in is the organizing impulse of his life, he knows, but how has he let it come to be so? And the problem is, he doesn't want to change.

"Nick, it's ready," Trish whispers up from the sitting room. She's pouring the tea as he joins her.

He asks her, "What do you think about when I'm fucking you?"

"I think about you fucking me. How you feel, how you smell."

"Do you remember things?"

"Sometimes. Mostly I just want it. I want it to be happening. That's what makes it desire, right?"

"Do you like it?"

"Or else I wouldn't do it."

"Will we always do it?"

Trish adds the sugar to Nick's tea. "No."

———

NICK DRIVES TO CAMPDEN HILL SQUARE, wondering at his foolishness. What game is he playing, getting her to talk about it? How fucked up is he? Why would he toy with his good thing? To make it stop, to free himself from its power? He doesn't want it to stop. This is what he's living for, that body, the surrendering of that body, its wet, its warm. This is the source of everything, of Charlotte, the force that makes her being possible, that gives Charlotte to the world so that he can exist to love her. And after he can't fuck Trish any more? He's known it will happen, and now she's said it.

He stopped fucking her once before, with no hope of fucking her again. Then, he was kicking a dirty drug, stepped-on. All that love and possession and romance to cut the potency. Now he's addicted to pharmaceutical grade, the pure her, the true commodity, its production controlled at the only source, by one who has no need to trade. What will be left? Only Charlotte, and his love for her—enough to crush them all under its weight. That love will never stop, but he'll stop. He'll cease to be.

What does she mean, they won't always? Will they stop because of the pregnancy? That's not what she means. It's what he would mean, how he would feel, but it bears no connection to any thought Trish could think. She does it because she likes it. What if it really is that simple for her? Yes, control; yes, greed; yes, her guilt assuaged. No doubt she's worked all that stuff out. But it's as she said. She does it because she likes it.

That's not how women are, or not how women have been taught to be. Maybe they'd all think that way and act that way if they were as evolved as she is. Yes, they all would. Then Johnny would fuck Con, Belinda would fuck—she'd still fuck Tommy. Grace would fuck—Nick, actually, poor old girl. And Sareen would fuck him too, but not only him. He should say a daily prayer of thanks that there is only one Trish, probably for centuries to come. It's not that she's a libertine, whatever that means this year, but something truly scary, a woman who can act on all her feelings. The glib thing to say is, just like a man, but men aren't like that. Some think they are and some, like Kess, wish they were. But feelings are not what drive the boys. It's lust for power, the acquisitional imperative, just basic alpha programming.

This is only the Trish in his mind. Trish to herself is not omnipotent. She thinks she's fucked up and confused, even if she doesn't show it. But in the great arc of anthropology, Nick knows his version of her is right. He thinks of Superman as a child, nearly deranged by powers he can neither explain nor deny, nor even find the means to measure. Poor Trish, my little Martian.


NICK WOULD PREFER NOT TO SEE JOHNNY, especially after the last time. He wouldn't mind if he could give and receive friendship, drink and curl up against the length of her, listen to her stupid tragic pain and tell her his. But he's too angry and too horny. He should eat something, and sleep, and then take a long time to sort through all the crap in his head, but instead he is up the stairs at Campden Hill Square and Johnny is kissing him hello. She's shopped for a cold supper. Nick asks if they can go out. He pleads jet lag: If we stay in I'll just crash. Let's keep moving.

They go to the Chinese place nearby. Nick keeps Johnny talking, not that she has anything to say. At least she isn't wired, like the last time. She suggests they go back for a hot bath and a bottle of Vesper.

"Fine, if you can do the CPR. How about a film?"

There's a horror picture at the Odeon on Ken High Street. Nick hates scary movies, in particular ones with imperiled children, but it beats the alternatives. Johnny settles her head on his shoulder, moving it discreetly every time he starts to snore. She's got sweets, a Coke, Nick asleep on her shoulder, a loud bloody mess on the screen in front of her—something American with pretty teenagers who you know are from television shows, you just don't know which. She's happy. Nick drifts between real and pretend sleep until it's over.

They walk back through quiet streets.

"I've really got to pee."

"Do it here. No one's around."

Johnny wonders if this will cheer him up. She holds on to an iron fence and squats on the sidewalk, her jeans around her boots. Nick keeps watch. She pulls her jeans up.

"Thanks for the nightcap."

"Are you OK, Nick? Really, are you?"

"I'm not great. Mostly just tired. You're being an angel."

"You're very low maintenance. Is there anything more I can do for you? Throw up? I'm a bit out of practice."

"No, but thanks. That might be next."


TRISH BRINGS CHARLOTTE OVER after Sunday lunch. They spend the afternoon playing. Trish leaves at about six. Nick is out of sorts. Charlotte is fussy, not unmanageable but in no mood to see Mummy go. Nick distracts her with some books and Charlotte pushes her Bunny around the flat in her stroller. She eats a decent dinner of steamed carrots and rice and gets to sleep, more easily than Nick expected, at eight-thirty. The evening has turned out OK. Nick focused because he had to and Charlotte, the mature one, responded. He sits with a cup of coffee and a plate of chocolate biscuits, glancing at a Spanish League match, trying to enjoy the presence of his sleeping child. He's angry with himself that he can't feel what he wants to feel most, can't escape the hamster wheel in his mind.

He remembers a condition he read about in a magazine, two flights ago. It was about people with a compulsion to eat things that aren't food: candle wax, metal, earth. Sometimes it's a sign of madness, sometimes the manifestation of a nutritional deficiency. Anemic women, particularly pregnant ones, have felt urges to eat red clay, which contains iron. Is his compulsion to eat Trish a way to get what he needs to survive, or is he just mad, hungry for her pencil shavings and china dust?

AS THE WEEK GOES ON he gets sadder about them leaving. On Tuesday, while Charlotte naps, Nick stands in front of Trish and opens his flies. Neither of them speaks, but their breathing is a conversation. Trish takes his hand in her hands. She kisses it and kisses his thumb and takes his thumb in her mouth and sucks it, her eyes not leaving his. She takes his dick from his pants. He thinks that he's going to cry, but he doesn't. This is what he needs, to be doing it after what they talked about, with the conversation still out in the room with them. What does it mean, that he feels so complete, that she closes over him like night?

Trish sucks his balls. They're what gave the possibility of Charlotte. Why, now that she senses this part of her life ending, does his dick feel so good, his balls, his muscled ass and thighs? It isn't nostalgia, he's got enough of that for both of them.

Nick puts his hands on her shoulders and she reclines, his lightest touch sufficient to move her, as if they were on the moon. She takes his clothes off to get more of him against her skin and in her hands. Nick fucks her with her knickers pulled to one side. He reaches under the elastic to hold her butt.

He pictures putting his finger against her asshole, pushing it into the glistening chapel to feel his dick fucking her. He pictures putting her lovely damp foot to his mouth and kissing the delicate toes with their lapsed blue polish. He pictures saying I love you.

IT'S CHRISTMAS EVE DAY, another afternoon in Kentish Town and another nap. This one is planned for, hoped for and waited for with honest shame by both of them. Trish puts Nick down on the bed and straddles him in reverse, working him with her hands and mouth. He raises his head to eat her. But he can't, he just beholds the sacred pussy, heaven's gate ajar before him. Charlotte begins to stir. Trish jacks him off into her mouth. Charlotte is crying and Trish is still naked and sticky when she picks her up out of the crib. Nick is flat on his bed, full of more than he can register. He can tell that this was the last time.

HE DRIVES OUT TO SEE GRACE AND MARCUS Christmas Eve. Mercifully, they do not notice or at least do not comment on the state of him. William is in residence with the new girlfriend, a grubby mouse who in the course of their long evening proves nasty as well—smug, judgmental, controlling. Her proprietary manner and lack of looks convince Nick that this will be the mother of his nieces and nephews. He imagines them, variously ugly, mendacious, and ill-tempered amalgams of Marcus and her. Tracy, that's her name, is however the only person to comment on Nick's unhingedness.

"You always like this then?"

"You're tired from all your traveling, aren't you?" offers Grace.

It wasn't even a fuck. She jacked him off. She serviced him. It was an act of some sort of communion, maybe, but mostly it was an act of mercy. Her last mercy fuck.

CHRISTMAS DAY, Nick wakes early and brings Charlotte and Trish back to Kentish Town. She has let him choose his time, and Nick goes for morning presents and Christmas lunch. He figures to see his girls fresh, but maybe it's just to get the ordeal over. A first proper Christmas with Charlotte, and it's got to be a trial. There are too many presents, from him and from Trish—colored plastic apparatuses that stack and slide and play tunes, stuffed animals, books, a stocking with oranges and toffee apple and cakes, Beanie Babies and snap beads. They go out for Christmas lunch, all dressed up, to the Grill Room at the Dorchester. Charlotte loves the turkey and the chipolatas. She meets her first profiteroles, waves to the waiters, and knows, from the glittering silver, shiny lights and banks of flowers, that it's a special day. Despite himself, Nick is barely there. This is a sham, and Nick feels bad, though Charlotte delights in the outing. Her only salvation is she's too little to get it.

After lunch they walk in Hyde Park, along the wide paths to the Serpentine and back. Trish points out birds and boats. Nick pushes the stroller. They walk around, like emigrés, because the local rites are unavailable to them. They walk to fill the time, to make a day of it. And the whole show is for his benefit. Charlotte should have music and crackers and a fire in the grate. She should peek into the kitchen to see what Mummy's cooking that smells so good. She should be in Islington, at home.

Trish reads Nick's mood and doesn't make it worse by trying to break through. To his relief, she just keeps it going with Charlotte. Soon this show will be over and Nick will drive them back and say goodbye and Charlotte and Trish will have their real Christmas. In the morning they will fly away. Parting will be intolerable, but it's all he can think of, and no harder than being together like this. Feeling like the gray of ten thousand Sundays, he shudders from the awareness that he's wishing this were over. Nick checks his watch and it's exactly when he thinks it is. The time moves no faster or slower than he's imagined. Each minute fills itself, drops and clears away for the next.

It must be just as bad for Trish. Except that for her what follows is relief, and reality. But Nick can't conceive of four o'clock from here, and it's already three-twenty.

He gets the car and they drive to Islington. Trish fills the air with talk of their return, to give Nick some kind of hope. A deep hug. Nick's cheek touches the velvet on the collar of Charlotte's coat as he kisses her neck. She smells of chipolata. He lets go of her into Trish's arms. His girls, or whatever they are, wave goodbye.

He turns the corner, pulls over, and sobs with emptiness. It's a sunny day in most parts of Britain, but here he sits, fifty yards from where Charlotte and Trish have passed through their portal into another, better Christmas. Nick stops crying. There's nothing to do but drive the car, just no place to drive it to. There is no one he wants to see and no one he wants seeing him. He goes back to Kentish Town, packs a bag and heads for Heathrow.

Nick feels less desperate on the M4. He reviews his options. New York? Turn it around and dump himself on the door of Kess or Tommy? Not Johnny, not right now. Steal into Zermatt and spend the week observing the happy family? Too Peter Sellers. At least the thought of this makes him laugh.

He gets a flight to Paris. It could have been Bombay, but he doesn't have the jabs, and he already keeps an Indian at home. It could have been Berlin, but he thinks he's past gestures. In Paris he can walk, eat and drink well, see lots of films—*version originale*. And if the idea stinks he can go somewhere else tomorrow.

TRISH AND CHARLOTTE walk through the door and into a house full of noise and cooking and family. Joe makes Trish hand Charlotte over to her mum and Maggie. He takes her upstairs and runs her a bath. He pours her a glass of champagne.

"Don't have one later then. You need one now."

He sponges her, tells her how tough it is, everything she has to deal with. He tells her how wise her efforts are, how kind and important. Trish finds she is weeping, for Charlotte and Nick and herself, from the strain of the day. Joe doesn't say more, he just strokes her head until it passes. He goes to bring Charlotte, who joins Mummy in the tub. That cheers her up. Their day washed clean, the girls join everyone for ham and turkey and more chipolatas. There is Christmas pudding, music and crackers, and a fire in the grate.

———

NICK ARRIVES AT CHARLES DE GAULLE after nine, and takes a taxi to the Sixth. He tries the Angleterre first, gets a sweet room, and starts drinking white wine in the brasserie downstairs. He finds a Tunisian place open nearby. His Christmas dinner is a decent couscous, washed down with Heineken. He goes through *Pariscope*, marking twenty hours' worth of film to see, and opens the Patrick O'Brian volume that has constituted his most recent dalliance with the printed word. He reads until late, drinking Calvados.

He wakes early on Boxing Day and settles into the bathtub, back in the war with Boney, and not hurting too bad. Part of it is knowing that he too is across the Channel, on the same land-mass as his little one, not so close as to invite self-contempt but closer than home. Part of it is the book. Part of it is the thought of a basket of croissants at Ladurée.

Nick speaks to no one but waiters, thinks of nothing, smokes too much, walks until his feet ache, sees two Billy Wilder movies and one new thing, scenic and violent, with Al Pacino. He drinks continuously—marc, Calva, Armagnac. He remains in a calibrated drunk the whole time, not sloppy but never sober enough to feel hung over, except first thing in the morning. He buys the next O'Brian book at FNAC, and a bunch of CDs he loves, even though he's got nothing to play them on. Some, Curtis Mayfield and War, he buys double, one for him and one for Kess, who'll remember. He has a number in his pocket—a good number, he was told. But he never rings it, jacking off to magazines instead. On the morning of the fourth day, with the anesthetic wearing off, Nick knows it's time to get back to London.

He tidies the flat and goes for a run. He calls Marcus and Grace and invites them in to visit with Charlotte when she's back. He phones Sareen, for the first time since Christmas Eve. He says he misses her, which is true as he's saying it. He tells her about Paris, hopes she had a better Christmas than he did, and tries not to be too hard to take. But he knows he must be awfully hard to take at this point.

ON NEW YEAR'S EVE, Nick and Koestler join Lucy and Johnny in Campden Hill Square. The evening's theme is America, in Nick's honor. The videos are *The Searchers*, *Sweet Smell of Success*, and *Goodfellas*, selected by Koestler. The girls do the dinner—fried chicken, mashed potatoes, apple pie. Nick brings bourbon and stuff to make whisky sours, but everyone agrees they're foul, so they drink the bourbon over ice with Coke. They eat too much and watch half of *The Searchers*, bored stupid.

"Big sky, endless film," says Lucy. "Can we switch?"

There are pop groups on Channel Four, which amuses Johnny and Lucy for a while. In the kitchen, Nick and Koestler pick up a conversation from the car.

"You're mad to worry. You've been seeing her for two bloody months. You can do anything you want."

"It feels longer."

"That's not good."

"No, maybe. Or else life feels longer. I've barely begun getting to know her."

"She's clearly the best woman you've ever stood a chance with. And those Indian girls are bred for it."

"I just met her at the wrong time."

"What movie are you from? Right, it's called *Trish*."

"It's complicated."

"When you meet someone while things are complicated, it

lets them get to know you. There isn't enough energy to maintain the front, so they see who's really there. If reality works, the odds are much better than if the reality is anyone's guess."

"You don't like Trish."

"No, but I fancy her. Surely that's got to qualify me for an opinion."

They switch to *Goodfellas*, which they've all seen and love. They are so engrossed that they only realize it's gone midnight when Johnny's mum rings. They're drunk, splayed out on top of each other—Koestler more conscientiously than the rest— Singapore and fourteen years having done nothing for his Lucy issues. Then they pop in *Sweet Smell of Success*.

"Why isn't New York like that now?" asks Johnny. "Nobody wears good suits any more."

"Marty Milner is Nick, and Burt Lancaster is Koestler, except you two like each other, for some reason."

Johnny feels Nick's hard-on through his pants, and brushes it, ineptly. Nick muses that understanding how unmusical this girl is would have saved him ten years of grief. The film and evening end. They stretch and scratch and bring ashtrays and plates down to the kitchen. Johnny asks Nick to stay. They stumble upstairs to Johnny's room, kissing on the way. Mistake, thinks Nick, but Johnny is in her Girl Guides mode, determined to get that tent-building badge despite a belly full of Maker's Mark. They undress each other. She may not be musical, but Christ, look at her.

Johnny goes down on him, unhelpfully. Nick pulls away, to reciprocate.

"Oh, I wouldn't. I'm just at the end of—"

Nick goes down on her. How long has he wanted to be here? The taste of iron—irony also, of course—but nothing more.

Johnny's face is off to the side, nodding like she doesn't know what nodding means. He fucks her, brings it all the way out, and comes as he jams back in again.

"So sorry. So drunk!" It's kind of a lie.

Johnny gets up to wash off. Nick looks at his penis. There's a cherry streak in the marbled glaze that coats it. Nick thinks: What I would have given, all these years, to have Johnny Colson's blood on my dick.

He allows himself not the luxury but the impertinence of falling asleep in their slime.


CHARLOTTE IS BACK FROM ZERMATT. Trish has her dressed in the velvet-collared coat, with a pink clip in her hair. Nick is moved and somehow surprised by how beautiful she is. But she looks smaller, poorly remembered, like a beach house from childhood. Marcus and Grace arrive in Kentish Town. They are happy that Charlotte recognizes them. Lunch is Nick's chicken and roast potatoes and cauliflower cheese, overseen by Grace, and edible. The store-bought trifle is a good one; great, by Charlotte's reckoning.


NICK IS ON THE FIRST FLIGHT to New York the next day, eager to make money, see Sareen and buy some gunmetal-gray suits with thinner lapels. He could stay out of England a long time, even with the usual ache over leaving Charlotte. He feels vague and empty. Has one part of his life ended for something else to begin in its place? Or will the emptiness, not unbearable, be the defining sensation of this new phase? Will these be the Empty Years? Is that too much to hope for, or not enough? He's seen three films in Paris, three on New Year's Eve, and now two more on the plane. Maybe these will be the Movie Years. Nick eats everything they put in front of him, uses both hot towels, and wears the little plane socks. But he drinks only Coca-Cola and coffee.

New York is dark and still, as commanding as a bereaved person about to speak. All its activity, commercial and social, is waged in refutation of the weather, and the central fact that this part of the planet just wants to sleep until spring. The false energy suits Nick, who has plenty of energy, all false.

He's geared up to see Sareen, but despite his hope and gratitude he finds he has nothing to say. When they go to bed he runs out of inspiration once he's toured her. He might as well be masturbating, and certainly she can tell. But Christ, it's so new. Or maybe it's just been convenient, and convenient to endow the thing with promise it doesn't hold. Sareen has stopped filling the gaps with thoughtfulness because she wants to see what's really there. On his fourth night back they meet for a late supper at Florent.

Sareen asks, "Are you OK?"

"As Bob says, 'It's life and life only.' "

"Bob?"

"Dylan. 'It's Alright, Ma.' From *Bringing It All Back Home*."

"What's the matter with you, Nick?"

"What's that supposed to mean?"

"We haven't been seeing each other that long, and I know you're mixed up. But I just don't have any idea what's happening here. Are we starting something, or what? I need . . . I expect some kind of effort."

Nick shrugs an apology.

"It's more than that. The connection is not happening. Not

when we talk, not when we go to bed. I'm sorry if I felt too much too fast. No, I'm not, but . . ."

"If it isn't working for you . . ."

What possessed him to steal her line? Is it wearing him out to think well of her?

"I'll pick up my things tomorrow afternoon. I'll leave the key."

"OK, but that isn't what I meant."

"You don't know what you mean."

Sareen is gone. Nick leaves his skate but he eats the fries on her plate, and finishes the wine.


WITHOUT SAREEN, he works more. Tommy comes through New York on the way to visit his sister in L.A. They go to Peter Luger and go to Scores. Tommy gets laid, of course. After three weeks Nick is due for a weekend home. It feels like a chore.

He goes to Islington to collect Charlotte. Trish really looks with child. Her white skin is rosy. Her smile is bigger, unguarded. Her voice is louder. He can't see the body under her yellow mac but he's sure it's thickened, not that she's any less adorable for it. She's like a big tea cake, delicious in ways he must have missed when she was pregnant the last time, on his sperm, when pain filtered all Trish information. Is this time different? He just sees her more.

Now she really belongs to Joe. It was a charge to fuck her when he knew she was carrying the jerk's kid, but that was just conceptual. Here she is, visibly given over to the primary purpose. It's universal, isn't it? When the female is showing, she goes into the off-duty tepee until the squirt is out. Everyone recognizes that a gestating female has no other significance. It's not a slur. The power of that miracle outweighs everything else. Nick still wants to fuck her, but doing so, or feeling bad about not doing so, just isn't on the menu this season.

For Trish also, it's different this time. The hormones have kicked in, so that she feels lighter the heavier she gets—justified, entitled, paid up. She is undistracted by guilt, except over Charlotte. Her dedication now is to their finite time alone. Mourning that private union is the only sad part, but she knows it will all work out. Harder things have.

Charlotte, at over thirteen months, is very engaged, chatty and smiley. She expects Nick's full attention. He carries her into the flat in Kentish Town and puts her down on the sitting-room floor. She stands up and follows him toward the kitchen. She's walking! Nick phones Trish: did she know?

"Yes, she walked after we got back from Zermatt. It's great, isn't it?"

"It's unreal. It's fantastic. Why didn't you tell me?"

"Wasn't this a good surprise?"

"Yes, incredible."

"Enjoy yourselves. Just know she gets into things faster than she used to."


BECAUSE MONDAY IS MARTIN LUTHER KING DAY in New York, Nick gets all of Sunday in London. He accepts an invitation to Islington for lunch. Somehow the pregnancy makes it OK for them to be there together under Joe's roof. A couple called George and Penny come round with their son Simon, one of Charlotte's playmates. Penny is blonde and jovial, but not stupid. George is in property. There must be men this boring eating lunch all over town right now.

Trish has asked Nick because it's a chance to see Charlotte with someone her own age. The kids don't exactly play together, although they approximate hugs of hello and goodbye when the adults steer them into it. They play side by side, aware of each other's presence and charged by it. They relate better to the grown-ups, offering their toys to the jury of big people.

Joe winces discreetly to indicate that these are not his friends. Smug fuck. He keeps throwing dry glances to say, let's share a laugh over poor whatever his name is. It's Joe's way of letting Nick know he's on the A list. And that's the second level of the con, because of course he's not. It's just funny if Nick's flattered enough to think he is.


CHARLOTTE COMES BACK to spend the night in Kentish Town. Nick watches her watch a Winnie the Pooh video, snuggled next to him on the sofa. He lives with missing her, and then every few weeks he gets to see her. He feeds her, changes her, bathes her and takes her for walks. He makes her laugh and holds her when she cries. He looks into her eyes and wonders what will become of them. He knows something, quite a bit, about her rhythms, her temperament, her sense of humor.

Today he got to see her at home, her real home, to see her relate to the adults and to Simon. She's still a baby but she's also a child now, and already a person, forever. He likes her a lot, a thing apart from his boundless love. What can he say about her? She's resolute and independent, like her Mum. She's mushy, like her Pa. She's quiet, but focused quiet. It doesn't take her long to warm up to people, but she doesn't warm up all the way unless she decides to, unless she likes them. She likes him. Will they be close? Is he ready to hear her? Is he ready to know her and let her in to know him? This is a miracle, a chance of chances, his daughter, programmed to love. Is he up to it?

There's a big to-do in the Hundred Acre Wood.

"Tigger's silly!" Nick laughs, and looks at Charlotte. Charlotte looks up sideways at Nick, and now she laughs too.

"Seely!"

A chance of chances.

ON THE PLANE TO NEW YORK, Nick wonders if he would dislike Joe under any circumstances, or if it's just the situation they must share. He wants to like him, though not as much as he likes to hate him. Joe's got his woman and his kid, which is reason enough for either feeling. Joe excels at smooth surfaces. He leaves no prints. That idiot father of Simon's didn't even realize he was getting lit up. The sincere questions delivered while fiddling with a wine glass—it was only sport, a bit of Sunday sadism, no blood drawn. Does Trish notice? That's Joe, she must think. He probably gets a lot of "that's Joe" working for him.

He reminds Nick of someone, an actor he can't place. It's the slouch, the false bumbling, that vast self-regard. He's sure it isn't coincidence. People must have noticed and told him, and then he started tuning it in. The short-sighted look, could be innocent, could be playing possum, until he breaks out of it like Mister Magoo at the end of the cartoon, and you're meant to understand that the whole thing was an Apollonian joke.

How much time does this bastard spend rearranging the furniture in Trish's head? And how much will he spend in Charlotte's, selling his truth and methodically undermining Nick's? It doesn't even matter to Joe. Take it, break it. Own or destroy. Charlotte will grow up feeling guilty for loving Joe too much and believing in Nick too little. And if he takes him on, he loses—maybe not during battle, but after, when Joe gets to rewrite, to spin it his way—and pity dumb old Dad.

How will Trish respond? Will she challenge Joe's crap? She's no zombie, and she certainly clocks what he's doing. But she'll tolerate it, within limits. She doesn't deny Joe anything. Oh yeah, except her fidelity.

THAT MONDAY NIGHT Trish does the washing up. Charlotte is asleep and Joe is out for the evening. She listens to the radio, singing along to Blondie. Joe doesn't understand it, "when we've got every CD in the world here. Wouldn't you rather choose for yourself?" But Trish likes being surprised. And even if she doesn't fancy a particular song, she likes to feel joined up, to know that other people are hearing the same thing she is.

"I will give you my finest hour, the one I spent watching you shower." Trish wonders if she's woken Charlotte. She pictures Joe naked and wet. Sometimes they're just boys, thin and straight, their skin all rosy from the steam. Sometimes they're such men, conspicuous, car alarms going off during church. What's really pervy is when they're both. Sexy boy, sexy man.

Joe was over the top at Sunday lunch, really bad. It was all for Nick's benefit—demonstrating his fangs to a rival, in the hide of some slow-moving prey. At least George didn't seem to notice. But Joe can be a not altogether nice person, and Nick gets it. Just as well, he needs to.

FEBRUARY IS ROUGH EVERYWHERE, but in New York at least there's some silver in the lead. Nick slogs away, glad for his bonus.

Johnny is coming to visit and he doesn't look forward to it. Things are complicated between them and all he feels is tired at the prospect of sorting it out. They haven't seen each other since New Year's Eve. Another woman he fucks who doesn't love him. Where to find the kind of girl who holds your face in her hands while she's kissing you? Oh yeah, he just broke up with one. Not fucking Johnny might be a good idea, but that isn't going to happen.

She arrives Friday evening. The world appears unnaturally darkened—the traffic, the slush, the airport and highway—like he's worn sunglasses by mistake. Johnny is manic with damaged joy. They ride into town, smooching, agent and double agent. Johnny showers. She runs into the living room, dripping, shivering and naked. All the promise of fourteen has been kept at twenty-nine. She is tall, but now perfectly proportioned, with flawless skin, a Cranach the Elder goddess. Just the way he always likes them, of course, because his taste was formed forever by love for this girl. And now the breasts are perfect too, not large, but full, rare arguments in gravity's defense.

And at last she is his. Johnny pulls him back to the shower like an adolescent grabbing the shy boy at a swing dance. Nick fucks her there, touching the perfection, drinking her mouth and the hot water that runs in and out of it. They are face to face, Johnny's back against the tiles as Nick rocks inside her. His hands rush to learn her legs and shoulders, taut and glorious, a god-damn race horse. It feels like their first true fuck, and Nick comes like a train. Johnny doesn't.

"Let's get you off."

"Later, OK? That was great. And I'm famished."

They go to the Post House and throw down rib eyes and Pichon-Longueville, laughing and talking, great friends, or new lovers, or something. They call a town car and go up to Jimmy's, dance execrably, and drink a lot of rum. Johnny gets a paper of blow from the driver to keep going. They ride home under sloppy kisses.

Johnny falls onto the sofa and pulls up her party frock, opening her legs to Nick. Such a big hungry rag doll. He grabs a handful of honey-colored hair to change the angle of her mouth. He kisses her, sucking her lips, banging his teeth against hers. She giggles at his Latin lover routine. What's in her head? Something sets a little sensor beeping inside him. Nick smiles and Johnny smiles back, straight into him: ancient, powerful, and his. Johnny's thinking a particular thought, and now he knows what it is.

Nick cuffs the side of her face. Johnny exhales and watches him. The little beeping sound gets louder. He's trying, drunkenly, to find a word. He searches for it, only to remember that of course he's already looked it up, quite recently.

Johnny says, "It's OK."

"What?"

"It's OK. It's good." Nick isn't getting it. Johnny keeps looking at him. "I like it."

Nick hits her again, open-handed, but harder. "I . . ."

"It's—I'm just a bit deaf, you know?"

Nick takes out his dick and puts Johnny's head down on it. She sputters a little, but sucks. He can feel tongue, teeth, throat. He pulls out of her mouth, raises her up by her ankles— those legs—and starts to fuck her. She's so ready. In and in and in. He takes a breast, squeezes the nipple and twists it hard. She stares into him. Her long body ripples in acquiescence. So many years of deflected desire. He wants to be here forever, fucking it, smacking it. Fuck, smack. He hits her with his free hand, palm side, and then back with the knuckle side. Johnny's head jerks sideways, her body still moving in waves beneath him. He hits her again. It's good. She isn't looking at him now. Her mouth is open. She is crying. Nick is coming. He sees that Johnny is crying but he keeps coming. He keeps hitting her. Johnny doesn't move away, she just ripples and cries.

Nick doesn't need to ask what he did wrong. Johnny won't speak. Her face is bruised, her lip is fat, and there's blood setting in one corner of her mouth. He brings her a bag of ice. She takes it and turns away. This is like the old days, not knowing her mind and caring desperately, only bleaker beyond imagining. Nick is lost about where he stands, with her and with himself.

Johnny goes into Nick's bedroom and closes the door. In a few hours it's morning, and Johnny emerges looking no better than before. She asks Nick to get her a car. It's a little after seven. He sits in the gray murk of his living room. I am the father of a daughter, he thinks. This is the end of my best friendship. And, he thinks, how am I going to get through the rest of the weekend?

In the next week, Nick leaves two phone messages at Campden Hill Square. He writes a letter but Johnny doesn't answer, so when he goes to London he doesn't call her. He sees Trish but avoids spending time with her. He takes Charlotte to Regent's Park. It's different, now that she's charging around like a baby Frankenstein, more work and more fun. At least it ought to be, but he can't tune her in.

Nick is still shaken. He mourns the friendship. It was—what?—a mistake, a catastrophe. The result of exhaustion, lust diverted? Not diverted—he came like Satan. Is he Satan? No—

this is her hang-up, not his. But he has discovered something new about himself. Maybe not that he desires it, because he doesn't. But he is capable of it. He knows because it happened.

It was something, to see her finally react. And that's who Johnny is, poor girl. She will never be happy. But he shouldn't have crossed into that part of her life. It wasn't worth finding out. By the way, will he ever be happy again?

What should he put it down to? How does he give it context? He was trying to get past her armor, to find some essence. Isn't that what she was doing too? He reassures himself that he isn't a monster. None of his explanations, rehearsed in an impersonation of rationality, add anything to the single searing fact of it. He hit her and it got him off. It wasn't murder, or rape, or the sad chimpanzee's tea party of S&M. It was this.

He won't discuss it with Koestler, who'd enjoy it too much. And anyway, Koestler must already know, from Johnny via Lucy. He shouldn't miss out. Koestler is an epicure of subjunctive moralities: who would or wouldn't hide a friend from the Gestapo, who could or couldn't support their family by driving the Belsen train. Even without Nazis, Koestler will get a lot out of this one.

Nick replays the scene, like a car accident, as though the details matter and might reveal a truth that means something. How many times did he hit her? Including everything, six, ten times? What was the quality of it? Not frenzy, more like a science experiment where the white coat gets the sedatives. Watching her face, watching her body move at last to his music, seeing her react, feel pleasure, curious at the sensation of each blow. It was a dream where you take your hand off the wheel and let the car cross to the oncoming lane. He found the depth of her. Johnny got what she wanted, to receive pain and then hate the giver. He's a monster and she's fucked up. Both of those things are true. He won't do that again, ever, to anyone.

But he jacks off to the memory. The way Johnny's whole body opened up to him as he hit her was a moment of true possession, the first time since before Trish that anyone's made him crazy like that. Anyone but her. Oh Trish. There's the girl he really wanted to hit. Such a sad thought. How long will he want her? Probably always.

WHEN SHE COMES BACK for a sleepover, Charlotte is fussy and clings to her Mum.

"She's teething."

Trish brings water-filled toys for Nick's freezer, acetaminophen, and some numbing gel that Charlotte knows and detests. She cries when Trish leaves but settles down pretty well over dinner. They watch *Spot* videos. Nick gives her a dropper of acetaminophen, reading the directions twice and checking the dosage with absurd or fatherly thoroughness. Charlotte rocks Baby and pushes her around the flat in her stroller. She takes off Baby's clothes. Baby joins Charlotte in the bath.

"Neh? Neh?" Charlotte is pointing at Nick. No, she's showing him her finger.

"What, honey?"

"Neh?"

At least one of them is clear on what the story is. Nick looks at Charlotte's pointed index finger. A little sliver of nail hangs off of it.

"Neh?"

"Oh, sorry, Duchess, I didn't see."

Nick looks around for a baby clipper or anything else that

would be safe to use. Charlotte stands up in the tub next to him. Her feet are planted under her reedy little body and her shoulders are back, like Popeye out on the town. Nick holds the offered finger up to his mouth and bites the nail gently, being careful not to take any more than is already detached. Charlotte watches with great interest, her eyes trying to peer after her finger right into Nick's mouth.

"All done!" Nick takes the bit of nail out of his mouth, feeling how small it is. "Unorthodox but effective."

Charlotte smiles at Daddy, because he is funny and because she is pleased that he wasn't too dumb to catch on.

She starts getting cranky again while Nick is dressing her for bed. He walks her around the flat, turning off most of the lights, patting her back and singing "All the Young Dudes," which comes to him from out of God knows where. He puts her down to sleep. She seems to go off, but then she rouses herself. This happens a second time. Nick tries walking her again but the crying ramps up. Another bottle, a toy from the freezer—no good. Charlotte gets through the squirming, wild-eyed stage, but settles into a resolute and unhappy sob.

"You don't need to suffer, little flower." Nick phones Trish.

"I'm glad you called. I wasn't sure she'd make it."

"Poor girl."

"I'll be over in a few."

"That's OK, the car's right here. Just keep an eye out for me."

Charlotte calms down in her seat. When she sees Trish she whimpers sleepily into her neck. She doesn't turn to Nick when he kisses her but is happy to let him touch the back of her head.

"Say 'Bye-bye, Daddy. We'll see you in the morning.' "

Charlotte says "Bye-bye," smiling demurely.

NICK TRIES TOMMY, who's game for a drink.

"Has my reputation suffered?" Nick says it lightly, but that isn't how he feels. He's sure Tommy's heard something about the Johnny business.

"Not in my circles. You'll have to ask your man Koestler."

"She's a good girl. I really fucked that up."

"You did, didn't you?" Tommy ponders a moment. "But it's got nothing to do with her being a good girl—though she is. As to you two falling out on her visit, the world assumes that you made declarations she could not return. It works better for her like that, do you see?"

"Works better for both of us. But if she isn't saying what went on, how do you know? You and I haven't discussed it, have we?"

"Don't forget I know Johnny."

"Well I guess her version is true, in a funny way."

"I don't think so," says Tommy.

"No?"

"She didn't spurn you because you thrashed her. You could be thrashing her still. She spurned you because you didn't like thrashing her."

Nick looks like he's swallowed a bad mussel.

Tommy continues, "You saw who Johnny really is, and she saw your reaction."

"But Tommy. I liked it."

"No, what you liked was finally knowing. You didn't like 'it'— you didn't like her." Tommy shakes his head and adds, "She's a sick old thing, but really very brave in her way. And as usual, she's the one who loses. Poor Johnny."

After the pub they go by the Beaufort Club. This is Nick's first time back since his wedding reception, but that's not what he's thinking about. He's thinking about finding something to fuck. And as he scans the garden, his gaze stops on a weathered blonde. It's Claire Porter, his first big crush, pre-Johnny. She went out with cuter, cooler boys than Nick, or anyone from Spencer. But she was happy to hang around with him when there was nothing better to do.

Claire was the one they all wanted, even before most of them had set eyes on her—such was her reputation. Nick first saw her at a party in Barnes, the summer of the year before O Levels. She was slight, brown-skinned, and tight as a drum. Drunk, playing badminton. It was like the first time seeing the Mona Lisa, through the crowds and the plate glass. Right, it's the Mona Lisa. You'd feel happy to walk off but you give it a moment and study the thing to see what the thing is, beyond what you walked up knowing already. It only took a minute for him to get it, the full shivering glory of her. He followed her inside, got her a drink and introduced himself with it. Take a number. She belonged to no one. The other girls parted for her convoy, the boys fell into her wake.

She was nearly feral. Saturday afternoons in the basement bedroom at her parents' house, listening to Side One of *Dark Side of the Moon*, or Sly Stone's "Sex Machine," making Nick sniff her armpits to see how hard she'd worked at a rehearsal for the dance recital. Saturday nights, a cloud of gin and Rive Gauche, grabbing Nick's only fare money and laughing as she burned it on the floor of a black cab hurtling toward Holland Park.

Once, she dared Nick to name someone she couldn't seduce, and he picked the father of a school friend, a professor at London University. After a short phone call at ten-thirty on a Sunday night—"I'm a friend of John's . . . Yes, the blonde girl . . . You're so distinguished . . . A man like you could teach me things"—they went to have a look. There the poor soul was, waiting for her outside the Gloucester Road tube station.

A few years later, straightened and chastened after her boyfriend's heroin bust, she sat naked on Nick's bed, a Degas pencil sketch of a surprisingly small girl.

This is Claire Porter, sixteen years older. She sees him looking at her and smiles short-sightedly.

"Claire!"

"Nick Clifford! How are you?"

They drink Scotch and exchange one-paragraph biographies. Claire has married well, popped two kids, eight and five. Now husband and daughters are in Scotland for the weekend. Neither asks after old acquaintances, they just take up another drunken evening in SW7. Claire is still very blonde and very brown. She's got some lines around her eyes—the bill for the drink and drugs and suntans starting to come due—but no fat, and he's wagering no cottage cheese. She's still the girl in the Donnie Elbert song—"A Little Piece of Leather." And still there's the cloud of Rive Gauche.

She invites him back to her house in Paulsen Square. Nick, to his own surprise, takes a pass, and asks if he can call her.

"Here's the mobile number. Daytime is best."


CHARLOTTE IS SITTING in something that looks like a chariot for mermaids, half-watching a *Teletubbies* video. Mostly she's paying attention to the jolly young lady with a pin through her nose who's cutting her hair off. Trish stands right next to Charlotte. She holds her hand and smiles at her reflection in the mirror.

"What a good time! Your very first haircut!"

"Yeh?" There's no mistaking the skepticism in those eyebrows.

"Just a little little bit."

It feels better when Mummy talks, because it always does, and now especially because it means the nose lady can't cluck at her.

"Good, almost done. Can we please be done soon, Julia?"

"Just a few snips."

"Nearly finished, poppet. What a good haircut getter you are. And now how about these pretty clips?"

The shiny things? Yes, please. One, two. And they don't hurt at all.

"Can you see yourself? Look how sparkly!"

It's over now, because she's out of the chariot and into Mum's arms.

"Here we go. Now what I think is, we ought to get something really yummy, like a big cake with jam, and lots of cream in it. What do you think?"

Mummy always knows what to do.


IN APRIL, Nick phones Sareen.

"I'm thinking of going to the islands for a few days. Would you like to come with me?"

"How are you doing, Nick?"

"I have no idea how I'm doing. I'm sorry you asked. How are you?"

"I've been fine."

"I was thinking five or six days. The week after next, or the week after that, if—"

"I don't think so."

"No?"

"Do you think you . . . ? Look, we tried. No thank you."

"It's a vacation. No trying. No trying allowed. I'll even carry your carry-on for you."

ON THEIR FIRST NIGHT they eat dinner at a Vietnamese place, upstairs in town. Walking to the car, Nick stops Sareen and kisses her. She takes his hand and they head for the line of palms. She pulls off her dress and falls to the beach, her body a dark S against the white of the sand. It's their only fast fuck all week.

They stay in a cottage and swim outside their front door. They drive into town to study the French fake hippies and try to figure out who's paired off with whom. They sleep a lot. They walk over to the western coves for picnics. They poke around the drugstore by the airport and eat a good cheap bistro lunch in the fly-infested courtyard, with the LIAT pilots. Nick smokes Havana cigars that he buys from a bandit with a shop in the village. Sareen writes in her notebook and reads a novel that Nick has never heard of, which isn't saying anything. They've got rhythm but no structure, which pleases them both.

Sareen is struck by Nick's love of the physical—body surfing, marching up hills. When he fetches a forgotten water bottle from the car, he trots off and sprints back, then storms into the sea to cool off. Nick loves how Sareen takes to the heat and sun and lambent water. She glides everywhere wearing nothing but a long cotton tee dress. Her neck bobs to whatever's playing,

Bob Marley or Vanessa Paradis, but she knows about music, holds strong opinions, and loves to argue them, unlike any woman he's known before. She never sweats. The mosquitoes fly past her to get to Nick.

Their sex begins unannounced, gathering its intensity and direction like weather. Nick smokes a joint and parts Sareen's legs as she naps in the afternoon. She doesn't move when she wakes up, except to open them a little wider. Feeling his eyes upon her, she swells and shines. The afternoon light has changed before they fuck, sitting on the bed, pressed together from their bellies to their mouths.

They stay an extra day. Still dressed for the beach, they take off over the bay at the end of the runway and sputter across to the large island where the jets land. Flying back, Nick imagines a wedding with Sareen's grandparents in Bombay, his father an embarrassment in white patent-leather loafers. Could he have that? What the hell is he thinking? He's thinking, could he have that. What does it say, that two months of sex and kindness from this big-hearted, food-cooking, back-rubbing beauty filled him with boredom and contempt? Now that she's away from all of that, and may not even like him any more, and consents only to be his groovy little fuck toy, he turns irredeemably romantic.

A MAN IS WATCHING TELEVISION when he hears a knock on his front door. He goes to open it and looks around. Nobody's there. He looks down and there's a snail on the mat. He picks up the snail and tosses it into the yard. About a year later, the man is sitting watching TV when he hears a knock. He opens the door and the snail's there. And the snail says, "What the hell was that all about?"

One of the guys at work tells this joke and Nick weeps with laughter. It's his own story. What the hell was that all about? How did it happen? What were the motives of those involved? Do the motives even matter, do they bear upon events, or does the shit just happen? That applies to him as much as anyone. When he reconstructs the chronology and traces how one thing led to another, he sympathizes with everyone's choices, even Trish's, even going back to Joe. But when he looks at each part discretely it makes no sense, and certainly no piece contains the blueprint of the whole design. What's up with everyone—him, Trish, Sareen? Only Johnny presents a clear outcome, clear and bad. And still a mystery, really.

Life proceeds, and work, and the deliverance of Daylight Savings Time. Nick gets a deal through the travel agent friend of an acquaintance, and he switches from BA to Virgin. Trish gets bigger. She breathes hard just moving around now, but she's happy. Charlotte is in love with Da. Any time he's not in her sight, it's "Da? Da DA?" all around the house. She cries when they say bye-bye. But she's a tyrant, determined to have her way over Mum, Dad, Marley, and the laws of physics. Nick calls her Scargill when she's at her most non-negotiable, and he loves the flair and fire of her. She may be a chain saw, but she's their chain saw. And she's always magnanimous in victory. Boy is your world about to get rocked, is what Nick keeps thinking.


NICK IS GETTING READY to go to the office on a hot May morning when Trish calls.

"Is everything OK?"

"Yes, fine. I'm just very close, lots of Braxton Hicks, so it's any day now."

"How's the girl?"

"Good, a bit fussy. I don't know if it's her sensing something or just where she's at."

Nick laughs. "She'll be more than sensing something soon enough, it sounds like."

"Yes. I wanted you to know where I'll be. I spoke to Grace, in case we need her to— But I want Charlotte to be around with us, so she's a part of it."

"And the info?"

"I've faxed it to your office. Let me know if it isn't there."

"How do you feel?" Nick asks.

"Oh, scared and excited. Complicated. It's definitely easier, having done it. I just— Sorry. I feel a bit disloyal."

"Well you are a bit disloyal, but not to Charlotte. Never to Charlotte."

Trish stops. "I love her so much. So everything."

"There's room. You'll see."

"Thanks, but how do you know?" she asks.

"I don't. I'd feel like shit if I were you. But then someone smart would say these things to me. And even if I didn't feel better I could hope that you were right."

"I hope you're right."

"Do your work, Trish. Charlotte gets to have a friend in the world. You don't know what it is, do you?"

"We don't. Well actually Joe does and I don't."

"You're kidding!"

"No. He wanted to know."

"And he kept the secret?" Nick is perversely impressed. "How good is he? No slips, no accidental pronouns?"

"He's good," Trish acknowledges.

"And you make a fine couple."

Trish recoils. "Are you being nasty? I can't even tell any more, but I haven't got the cushion for it."

"I am being nasty, but I'll stop. We have our whole lives to be nasty."

"I suppose that's really tender of you, darling."

"I thought so. Trish? Everything about you will always be difficult for me. But I wish you well. Not only for Charlotte, but that too, that mainly."

"Thank you." Trish goes on, thoughtfully. "That's just who you are, isn't it? After everything, with everything, you still wish me well."

"Hmm."

It's the beginning of something and the end of lots of other things. The end of hope, at least that hope, the end of a possibility, the end of Charlotte's perfect universe, or as perfect as it could ever be. On to something better, no doubt, but a different country, one she has no idea she's about to inhabit. *Goodnight moon, goodnight mush. Goodnight nobody.*


TWO DAYS LATER, Trish is in labor. It's another professional performance, with updates from Trish's mum. After fourteen hours Charlotte has her co-star, a healthy boy named Christian Somerville. Nick speaks with Charlotte a number of times—she sounds excited, aware of the commotion, receiving attention, not yet spooked.

When he visits, Nick notices a change in Charlotte's play. The idea of falsehood, that there are layers of communication to discern and control, begins with peek-a-boo. Life teaches that these skills can be used in pursuit of power: Mummy plays bait and switch, substituting a favorite toy for the newly discovered pair of scissors; Daddy absorbs baby in a storybook while Mummy slips out to the market. At first there are no hard feelings. Mummy returns with kisses and cakes, and everyone shares in the victory of reunion. But soon memory improves, scores are kept, and Mummy's return is greeted differently—by a squirming refusal to celebrate one's own gullibility. Later, but not by much, baby learns to dissemble: she allows herself to be wooed to the party, exacting three biscuits as reparation instead of the one that's been offered.

All of Charlotte's actions have a new edge, the concept of zero-sum having entered her consciousness. Every game—getting the loose knob off the stove, or the shaving foam out of the cupboard by the bath—is defined by its outcome, the reality of a winner and a loser. And Nick, like most reasonable parents, uses a lifetime of experience to accommodate the shift and, whenever safety permits, to embrace the role of a good loser. So even though Charlotte isn't allowed to pull the knob off the stove, Nick rewards her with mock consternation when she filches his mobile phone from his shirt pocket. It's much more interesting than being given it.

It would have happened anyway, but the presence of a rival—a new magnet for the grown-ups, one with the remarkable power to command food from Mummy's body—is an accelerator. I'm with you, friend, thinks Nick. I don't get those tits any more either.

Now Charlotte does not like being away from the theater of war. It's OK when Mummy and Christian come with Charlotte to Da's on Saturday morning, but truly grand when Mummy and Charlotte arrive alone on Sunday, leaving the turnip with Joe. Both times, Charlotte lavishes Nick with love, though on Saturday her peripheral vision is heavily engaged. Surely Mummy can see all the neat things that distinguish the walking, talking, flirting Charlotte from a turnip.

On Sunday night Nick goes over to Islington with the girls, obliged to see Joe in his glory. A master dissembler, that one: modest, mature, loving to all, magnanimous in what only his posture reveals as total victory. It's the most engaged that Nick has seen Joe with Charlotte, no doubt to display the fairness of his love for both children. Nick can't like it, however much he appreciates that the gesture is for his benefit, and Charlotte's— for the losers in the game. But he also sees that the two really like each other. Joe gets Charlotte, he gets her vibe. He finds her dear, funny, clever. Charlotte will need that. Thank goodness they didn't have another girl.

Nick even feels better about his own failings. It was something Grace said regarding Trish: "Have some understanding. It's hard to spend long hours alone with a very young child." Nick has reproached himself for being tired, or distracted, or cranky, for not always rising to his best after flying so far and spending so much to be with Charlotte. If he resents Trish, even if he resents Charlotte, if it's just tough sometimes to stay focused and forget his own miseries, at least admitting to it makes things better. That and reminding himself that it was his choice, his indulgence, to go live in New York.

ON A SATURDAY AFTERNOON in June, Nick is back where he doesn't want to be: the sitting room in Islington, waiting for Charlotte to return. She is out with Trish and Christian, and expected back. It leaves Nick alone with Joe, a thing that has befallen him only once before. Joe is languid and hostly, bringing beers for the two of them. But his eyes shine, and a tight grin works to keep control of his face. There's a lot of energy here to-day, eager to cut its way out.

He wants to fuck with me, thinks Nick, as Joe asks him about New York and how he finds it. A stupider antagonist would look to top Nick's observations, but Joe is a subtle player. Although he listens and questions with an interest that is cor-rect in its particulars and beyond reproach, Nick knows that the hot smiling eyes are all contempt. He hopes for everyone's sake that Joe can contain it, because he would truly love to thump this weasel, smash his head against the uneven edges of all those handsome bricks around the fireplace.

Joe opines, "You know, you're absolutely right. Of course, I've never lived there. But whenever people talk about how in-tense New York is, I always wonder what they're on about. London strikes me as far more tiring—the traffic, the inconve-nience. Even the air is heavy and uncommitted here. New York seems very doable, by comparison. And the weather there may have more extremes, but at least it's clear—like the Americans. Or am I full of shit?"

"No, I think you're right," says Nick. "By the way, this is a perfect beer for the weather."

"I'm not big on French beers, but yes, it's just right for this kind of afternoon. Unserious."

"So how's it all going?" Nick ventures. "You've got quite a full house now."

"Oh, it's great. Christian's still just a grub, but it keeps Trish busy. And Charlotte—well, I don't have to tell you."

"How do you find she's adjusting?"

"Well it's funny, Nick. The first week or two she was mostly stunned. At the beginning she was curious, tentative—'Who is this? What is Mummy doing all the time?'—and then once she started to get it you could see she was just gobsmacked, eyes as big as saucers, taking it all in. Trish as you know is fantastic, hands Christian off to me and whomever, really protects her time for being close with Charlotte. But it's not the same. You wouldn't have to be as smart as that one is, to know it. So for most of the first month she's been shocked, just clocking it all. Too quiet, too sweet, poor thing. And still, it's all a part of life, I tell myself.

"But in the last, oh, just the last week, or even less—it's changed. She's bolshy now. 'Dat.' 'Mine.' 'No no no.' Proper tantrums, back arched—the full Freddie Mercury, I call it. Of course, that's also the age, they say. The terrible twos, just starting early."

"Is she unhappy?" Nick asks.

"Well I fucking would be, wouldn't you? Displaced by the new toy. And she can dream, but she must know, deep down, that he isn't ever going to go away."

"As you say, it's a part of life."

Joe has the look of a striker setting up a free kick. "I—I'm sorry, was that insensitive of me? How are you doing, with everything?"

"I'm getting on with it. I'm fine."

"Good. But . . . Look, Nick, I'm sure you don't want to talk about personal things, and no doubt I'm the last person on earth you'd be doing it with, naturally. I just mean, you don't have to be fine. I've seen enough of you to know that you will be, even if you aren't yet."

What is it with this cocksucker? Did he and Trish have a fight? Maybe she's cleared off for the afternoon, leaving him locked and loaded with no one to blast. Not that Nick can entirely picture it. He and Trish never had a fight. At least Trish never fought back. So yes, he could imagine her pissed off enough to bolt with the kids, but not enough to give the little shit some of his own back.

"Thanks, no. I don't fancy reviewing my inner workings with you." Nick wants to end it here.

"Oh God, I've offended you yet again. I wish you could see it just once from my side—how I put up with you, knowing you're aching to take a swing at me the whole time. I don't blame you. But what's the point of being angry with me? It's her you should be angry with."

Nick answers with exaggerated evenness. "I am angry with her. But I also like her, God help me. You can understand that, I hope. But I don't like you. I try not to make a problem of it, but I don't. Never have. You and I could have met anywhere, under any circumstances, in any century of human history, and I would still want to see you dead. You're a self-satisfied bastard. And I know you hate me too."

"I'm not bothered. But I respect your honesty, Nick, though you aren't telling me anything new. And no, I don't think I'd hate you under other circumstances. As blinded as you are by your own pain, I don't expect you to see it, but I don't hate you at all. Even now."

"No?"

"What is there to hate?" Joe likes the sound of it. "What is there to hate? I won, you lost. Actually, you were never in the game. You just didn't know it. So you didn't lose the contest. You lost the prize."

"The prize? Trish?"

"Trish, Charlotte most of all. Your little girl! Your life together as a happy family the way you imagined it would be. And had every right to. The product was improperly labeled. If she were a can of soup, you could sue."

Nick doesn't believe they're doing this. "Are you trying to be a cunt, or is this really the way you think?"

"I'm warming to the topic. Nice day, nice beer, we're finally having our sit down. We're about due to clear the air, don't you think?"

Nick stares at him. "No, I don't think."

Joe bulls on. "Manners would normally prevent us, but it's just us two, right? I mean, Trish is something special. That's knowledge we're both privileged to share. Capable, resilient. Hot as a pistol. She always has been. Open like a spring flower, just wants to fuck all the time. That, and all those other charming specialities of hers. I've never met a girl who's like her. She's a dirty thing, and totally at home with it. That's the beauty of Trish. She wants to do all the nasty stuff that men want to do to her. She wants to. Not like other women, surrendering their dignity to prove they love a man. Trish just wants it, same as us. So she's magic. And the fantastic thing is, because she wants it, her dignity is intact, perfectly intact. And we're the jabbering fools. Am I wrong?"

"I don't get you. What are you trying to do?"

"Provoke a conversation, Nick."

"Why?"

"I'm doing you a favor. Maybe if we get some of this stuff out there, you, me, Trish, maybe you'll stop acting so . . . tortured."

"I am tortured. It is torture. I fell in love, you came back, and—boom—she just goes. And I don't understand, so I'm tortured."

Joe barely hears him. "Understand? Let me see if I can help

you. This is the thing about girls like Trish. You're the type to worry about her, about her happiness. I don't. I respect her ability to look after herself, and I get on with looking after me. That—listen to what I'm saying, now—that is how adults are supposed to behave. I know Trish. You haven't got a clue. Trish is a giver. And she needs a man who knows what a filthy little whore she is, who's secure enough to accept it and appreciate it and take some more of what she needs taken. It's the only form of 'thank you' that matters to her. Which is what I *understand*, and you do not. Which is why I'm the one who tucks your daughter into bed at night."

Nick stops in order to think, but he knows he doesn't want to any more. "I say thank you all the time. I did it the night after she went back to you, and then after Charlotte was born, every bloody weekend in my flat. And after she was pregnant with Christian? Then too. Then too. Like the fucking Beatles, 'Here there and everywhere.' I've said thank you again and again and again. The girl just can't get enough of 'thank you.'"

"Pardon?"

"You're the one who knows her so well, Joe, you tell me. Here's a thought: I wonder if you think it's all been about you. But you must know I don't give a toss. It was better revenge that you didn't know. And from Trish's side? Sorry, chief. From the looks of her, I'm pretty sure she wasn't thinking about you either."

Nick is rolling now. "Or maybe you think it's about the pussy. Yes, the pussy is great, agreed. And the mouth, and the bum. Her specialities, as you put it. So of course it was about that. But it was also about some obviously, clearly pathetic dream I had that maybe I could get her back. The pregnancy threw me, but then I thought, how do I know it isn't mine? Because Trish says so? She would, wouldn't she, whoever's kid he is. That's something else we both know about her.

"It doesn't matter though, because now that Christian is here, I can see that you will never go away and Trish will never leave you to come back to me. So in spite of the small consolation of how fucked you are, and the bigger one of how I've been doing her for the last year, you win. You win."

"I know." Nothing moves. Joe continues, "What you told me. Trish told me. About you two."

"When?"

Joe looks at a corner of the carpet that needs sewing. "Recently."

"Why?"

"It isn't your fucking business why! But she isn't going back to you, if that's what you're thinking."

Nick drinks his beer, unable to add it up.

"She knows if it happens again I'm gone. And that I'll make a point to take my boy with me."

"But you still want her?"

Joe looks at him. "Yes. Don't you?"

It's probably only a few minutes until they hear the latch. Trish comes upstairs quietly, holding Christian, who's conked out.

"Charlotte's asleep in the stroller. I see you've talked. Nick—"

Nick looks at her like a boxer trying to focus his corner man's face.

"—maybe you should come back. I'll ring?"

Nick goes downstairs. At the door is the stroller, and in it is Charlotte, in her jeans and sandals and a sleeveless pink polo shirt, head back, mouth open, sleeping serenely. He bends down and inhales her sweetness, the smell of the park on her. Should I take her out of here, just carry her away from all the sickness, right now? No. Trish will manage this. Actually she already has.

As soon as he closes the door behind him, Nick knows he isn't done. Is it the awareness that his girl is there, just behind the heavy oak? Or the feeling that he doesn't want to be handled any more?

Nick taps the metal knocker, distinctly but not loud. Tap tap tap. He's picturing their faces upstairs. Tap tap tap. Footsteps descending. The door opens. It's Joe—surprised, not surprised, his armor removed. Joe, shattered. They exchange a weird little acknowledgment, and Nick tries to think in the few seconds it takes them to walk up to the sitting room. Do I sympathize with him? That's going a bit far, but fuck, he looks awful. Like me.

Trish is not happy to see him. "Can I get you something?"

Nick sits down in the big chair. "I'm trying to grasp what happened today. I'm trying to grasp the last two years."

The noise of a moped through the open windows. She wants him to go.

Nick says, "You wanted the best for everyone, Trish. I know you did. Starting with yourself, but don't we all? Joe—you ruined my life. You get Trish. You're fucked, and still I'd trade with you."

Nick looks at Trish. "I haven't stopped loving you. I never will."

"Why?" Joe asks. Joe, who caused the crash. And now it's his world, it's Joe that won't ever recover.

Nick explains, "You made me feel that you were mine completely, the way no one else had ever been. Of course you were never mine. So I must have felt that too."

Joe is standing in front of the door. "Let's hear what the cunt has to say."

Trish hisses back, "I don't want any part of this. I've explained myself to you—and only to you. I've apologized to everyone. Fine, I'm evil. Bitch, cunt, whore. Now fuck off."

Nick experiences a moment of lightness, relief at not being the one fired upon. And immediately, in the lightness, he glimpses something ugly, knotted, hideously painful if you touched it. The glimpse passes, but he'll remember that he saw it. What? The thing that we are born with, that we are attached to and fed by our whole lives. The pain of everything, mundane, inescapable, delivered with us like a second placenta, from which we cannot be cut and still survive. How, for him, did Trish become its bearer?

Nick stands up.

"See you soon," says Joe.

Nick goes, and Trish follows him downstairs. At the door he turns to her. Trish's eyes fill with tears. She looks from Nick to Charlotte.

"Christ, I've made a mess."

"But not of her. We haven't done that yet."


THINGS CHANGE. Nick collects Charlotte or Trish drops her off at his door. Nick wonders if they'll talk about it. Maybe years from now, or maybe never. How did it happen? Did Joe suspect, and badger her? He is quite the badger. Did she use it, angry over something else? That's not Trish. She brought it up on purpose to close the book, remove the threat. She's practical enough. So Nick rose to the bait and betrayed Trish to Joe, who knew already. Although maybe he didn't know all of it until Nick told him. He can't help but admire the architecture of the thing, even if it didn't play out quite as she planned.

Is he angry with Trish for orchestrating the set-up and walking him into it? Is Trish angry with him for selling her out? He thinks that maybe nobody's angry with anybody, except for Joe, who is angry with everybody, and now with good reason.

He has to trust that Joe will not make Charlotte pay for it, or in any case that Trish will protect her. Trust, but verify, as the arms negotiators used to say. He'll have one more thing to worry about her over, whatever good it will do. He isn't angry with himself. He's had a long season of being angry with himself, and it's led to nothing but shitty behavior. That's what happens when you love and lose.

A benediction: let's try to move on. Nick's got his whole life to miss having Trish and fucking Trish. The sum he can't do in his head or on paper, the one for which all the other hurts are wall shadows, is the hurt of Charlotte.

SHE'S STILL IN LOVE WITH TELEPHONES: toy phones, cordless phones, mobile phones. She conducts long conversations in her strange-sounding slur, careening around the place, often with one on each ear, like a bookie. The television remote, a hairbrush, a piece of toast—anything oblong gets shouted into by this child. She is less patient with real phone calls, where she can only control one side of the dialogue, but that is usually how Nick enters her day, and almost always her bed time.

This is a girl who is not happy when crossed, and sometimes not happy at all. Her tantrums blow through like an atmospheric disturbance. When Trish or Nick sees one coming, it's steered into rather than avoided, the quicker to get to the other side, to clarity, equanimity, sun.

Nick spends the weekends in England with Charlotte, in

Kentish Town or visiting Grace and Marcus. He gets up to the Cooper's Arms from time to time, but Gorman and Tate aren't around as often. He sees Tommy. Koestler's not back from Singapore yet. He doesn't call Johnny any more.

Charlotte is no longer a subject for interpretation. She's a little person full of big opinions. With "please," "no," and "more," she may not always get her way, but she tolerates no mystery over what that way is. And she's so much fun. Da means protection, and adoration, but most of all he means excitement. Even going to the supermarket: Nick finds an empty aisle, pushes the cart away ahead of him, and hollers, "Runaway maiden!" Charlotte screams with laughter as he catches her up, colliding into her outstretched arms and kisses. Now she knows that bye-bye lasts a long time, so that when she goes back to Trish she mostly hides her face in Mum, unable to look back at her sugar bear.

IN SEPTEMBER, Nick proposes a plan to Trish: he'd like to bring Charlotte to New York for a long weekend. Halloween falls on a Sunday. He could come at the weekend to visit, bring her over, then return with her, Saturday to Monday.

Charlotte sleeps over for two nights in Kentish Town in September, as kind of a dry run. Trish says let's see how she's doing nearer the time; but it seems all right.

Grace wonders at the jet lag. "Will you even be able to see straight?"

Trish says, won't it cost a packet? It's only miles. Yes, 240,000 of them. But he's having a good year.

Sareen cooks for a day at Nick's apartment, freezing meals for them in case they want to eat in. Nick explains that Charlotte likes pasta, frozen peas, raisins and chocolate milk. The pot pies and pasandas are dear but unnecessary. Sareen just wants to do it. She doesn't think she should be around. Nick says they'll play it by ear, and he agrees with Sareen that she won't stay over. Nick fills his room with toys and buys a portable crib.

Nick and Charlotte show up at Heathrow with a lot of Kentish Town and a fair bit of Islington in their luggage, all to make things familiar. Charlotte can tell it's an adventure. Trish has her dressed up, as in the old days of air travel.

The plane leaves at three, but Charlotte stays awake. She clambers and plays and watches cartoons in her car seat. He worries about the headphones so he keeps the sound low. Anyway they don't stay on for long. The flight attendants are all beside themselves, doting upon the adorable daughter and her tender sexy dad. I'd have my pick, Nick thinks. He explains how that's what Mummy used to do.

"Mummy! Mummy bye-bye."

Late in the flight, after its endless autumn sunset, Charlotte falls asleep beside him. What should I do, Nick wonders. What about? Things have worked out, haven't they, to the extent that things ever will? Her head is to one side. He observes her curls against the angelic cheek, the purity of nose and lips, the capacity for obstinacy still evident in the sleeping jaw.

It's time to go back to London. Sit down with Evan, figure it out with Sareen. If there's no job in London I'll find a new one, but I've got to be home. By Christmas, home. This beautiful flower grows there, in the wreckage we made, and she thrives. I've been trying to have it both ways—peace, I'll convict myself later. Now it's time to go back, to live where Charlotte must, and make it be right. To thrive too if I can.

CHARLOTTE FALLS ASLEEP AGAIN in the town car and stays asleep into the apartment and through the night. When she wakes, at four-thirty, the room is full of her things, old and new. The apartment is ripe for exploration. It's got plenty of phones.

At six they go around the corner to the twenty-four-hour coffee shop for breakfast. The guys on the early crew are delighted to meet Nick's daughter, and they make a fuss. Charlotte eats part of the white of a boiled egg, part of a vanilla yogurt, part of a banana, some Cheerios and some chocolate milk.

They return to the apartment. Nick gives Charlotte a bath. She cries when he rinses off the shampoo under the shower head. Then Nick has a shower while Charlotte plays at the other end of the tub.

"Pee pee!" She points. She's seen him naked before. Nick is always fairly discreet about it, but he doesn't want to make it a mystery for her by hiding himself. "Pee pee?" It's a long story, he thinks, lifelong

"Daddy pee pee!"

"Yes, Daddy's pee pee. All done! Now let's get dry and toasty."

They watch *Teletubbies* and half of *Sesame Street*, and head out to Central Park. They ride on the merry-go-round. Charlotte sits on her horse and Nick stands next to her. She holds on to his waist, face against his belly, laughing. Next is the Children's Zoo. Charlotte is sleeping in his arms when Nick goes back across the park with his little flower, his sturdy little flower.

He phones Trish to report, and Sareen, to come over. Charlotte is still asleep when she arrives. When they hear her stirring

Sareen leaves, to come back in half an hour, so that Charlotte can grant her admission to their realm. She's busy checking the telephones when the buzzer sounds. Nick makes formal introductions and stays close by. But Charlotte takes to Sareen at once. Maybe it's just the softness of a woman. Charlotte eats some raisins, and discovers string cheese.

It's time to dress for Halloween. Nick has bought her a bee costume—tail, antennae, a black and yellow striped pod. She wears it over black tights and a black turtleneck. Charlotte doesn't get the bee part, just that it's funny and special, which is plenty. She loves all of it, except for the antennae. Nick wears fluffy pink bunny ears, which Charlotte endorses.

"Should I defrost something?" Sareen asks.

"Let's have a go with the lamb pasanda. There's always takeout, if that doesn't work."

"Is the lamb pasanda for her or for you?"

"I'm a bad, selfish man, it's true. She'll be fine."

Nick and Charlotte head to Sixty-ninth Street, which the police have closed to traffic. Most of the buildings feature elaborate Halloween decorations. Others have turned their lobbies into haunted houses for the kids to explore. Some stage little plays on their front steps. The street teems with costumed children, trick-or-treating for shopping bags full of candy.

Nick is in his bunny ears and Charlotte in her bee costume, sans antennae. Charlotte, in his arms, stares amazed from person to person, strange get-up to strange get-up, noticing many other little ones in parents' arms or on their shoulders. Nick takes her into a few buildings. Some are running smoke machines, the cold fog lit green or red or orange; some play spooky sound-effects tapes. Charlotte is more bemused than frightened by any of it, but she's got a hawk eye for the sweets.

"Dere? Dere?"

"Yes, let's go there, and see that lady. What do we say?"

"Piece? Dere!"

"Well, it's meant to be 'trick or treat.' But 'please there' works too."

Charlotte smiles when she sees her fractured reflection in a well-broken mirror. Does she realize that she's a part of the show and not just the audience for it?

"What does a bee say? Do you know? You're a little bee, you know. You say bzzzz."

"Eh?"

"You say bzzzz."

"Zzzz."

"Yes, that's it!"

Charlotte grins a loopy toothy grin. "Zzzz! Zzzz! Bee!"

"There you go!"

Charlotte's starting to look a bit glazed, but she complains when he tries to leave the block. Nick holds her close, face out, with her body against his chest, even though she really isn't cold in the costume. She kicks Nick every time he stops. It's like a hallucination in front of her, and she wants Daddy to keep it rolling. He waits her out, and she doesn't complain when Nick turns a second time onto Columbus.

They are booked on a morning flight to London and Nick wants her to get a good night's sleep. Sareen has the rice and salad and lamb pasanda ready. They sit Charlotte in her bee out-fit on the sassy seat. She takes a few bites. She likes the creamy lamb that Nick mashes up after segregating the bits of almond. She eats a few handfuls of rice. What the kid wants is to sleep. Nick brings her into the bedroom, changes her diaper and gives her a bottle. She's out in half a dozen swigs.

He comes back to the dining room. Sareen stands by the table, smiling—with her mouth, her eyes, her body, hair. Every cell of Sareen is smiling.

"Hi, Daddy. Are you still hungry?"

"Yes."

Nick is smiling too. He comes over to her, to this goodness, this good person. He pulls her close and kisses her. It's a fine moment, as fine as any moment has been for a long time. It won't last, but Nick thinks maybe there will be others, for all of them.

## ACKNOWLEDGMENTS

Thank you to everyone who read and improved this story—in particular my beloved, Ana-Rosa, and my friend Hooman Majd. Thank you, David Gernert and Erin Hosier. Thank you, Nan Talese, for your clarity and passion.

And thank you, Brian Koppelman.

DAVITT SIGERSON grew up in New York and London, and read history at Oxford University. He has worked as a songwriter, record producer, and journalist, and as an executive in the music business. He lives in New York with his wife and their two daughters. He is working on his second novel.

A NOTE ABOUT THE TYPE

This book was set in a digital version of Fairfield Light, designed by Rudolph Ruzicka (1883–1978) for Linotype in 1940. Ruzicka was a Czechoslovakian-American wood and metal engraver, artist, and book illustrator. Although Fairfield recalls the modern typefaces of Bodoni and Didot, it has a distinctly twentieth-century look, a slightly decorative contemporary typeface with old-style characteristics.